THE CASE OF THE
BROKENHEARTED BULLDOG

A Thousand Islands Doggy Inn Mystery

B.R. SNOW

This book is a work of fiction. Names, characters, places and events are either used fictitiously or are the product of the author's imagination. All rights reserved, including the right to reproduce this book, or portions thereof, in any form. No part of this text may be reproduced, transmitted, downloaded, decompiled, or stored in or introduced into any information storage and retrieval system, in any form by any means, whether electronic or mechanical without the express written consent of the author. The scanning, uploading, and distribution of this book via the Internet or any other means without the permission of the publisher are illegal and punishable by law.

Copyright © 2016 B.R. Snow
ISBN: 978-1-942691-06-8

Website: www.brsnow.net/
Twitter: @BernSnow
Facebook:facebook.com/bernsnow

Cover Design: Reggie Cullen
Cover Photo: James R. Miller

Other Books by B.R. Snow

The Thousand Island Doggy Inn Mysteries

- The Case of the Abandoned Aussie

The Damaged Po$$e Series

- American Midnight
- Larrikin Gene
- Sneaker World
- Summerman
- The Duplicates

Other books

- Divorce Hotel
- Either Ore

To Laurie and Stella

Chapter 1

I stretched out on one of the lounge chairs surrounding the massive swimming pool. Being late September, the pool was empty, and I knew that after this annual end of summer soiree ended, the pool would be covered and the lounge chairs stored away until May. Or if winter behaved like the last person at a party who refused to take the hint and leave, the chairs might not make another appearance until June.

Chloe, my gorgeous Australian Shepherd Josie and I had rescued from the River a few months ago, took my prone position as an invitation to climb up on my full stomach and stretch out. I groaned from her weight, but couldn't say no to her. I pulled myself into more or less an upright position and Chloe took the hint, moved down, and repositioned herself until she was draped over my legs. She propped her head on top of her crossed front paws and surveyed the scene.

A couple of hundred people filled the lawn of the Clay Bay Yacht Club. It was an interesting mix of locals, summer residents, and boat owners and their crew about to depart for warmer climates. Dozens of dogs mingled through the crowd on the prowl for food and friendship. I surveyed the scene and reviewed my notes for the speech I had to make later. I hated public speaking more than just about anything, but since John Gordon, owner of Gordon Yachts and president of the Clay Bay Yacht Club, always included a fundraising component for the Thousand Islands Doggy Inn rescue program as part of his annual end of summer party, it was the least I could do.

This year, John had donated a brand new fishing boat that retailed north of a hundred thousand dollars. And all summer people had been buying five dollar raffle tickets for a chance at winning it. As of this morning, the total number of tickets sold hit the thirty thousand mark. A hundred and fifty thousand dollars would shelter and feed a lot of dogs, and we owed John big time. A three-minute speech to thank him for all his support barely scratched the surface.

But that didn't make the thought of speaking in public any more appealing. Or less frightening. I shuffled my note cards, put them back in my pocket, and stroked Chloe's head. She closed her eyes, and I was about to do the same when Josie, my best friend and business partner, wandered in my direction.

As always, every pair of eyes she walked past followed her movements. A man I didn't recognize continued to stare at Josie as he walked with his wife along the edge of the pool and *almost* fell in. His wife grabbed his sleeve at the last minute, and he successfully windmilled his arms until he caught his balance. She seemed to regret saving him from the cold water because she scowled and left her embarrassed husband standing by himself.

I stifled my laughter, but Josie hadn't seen any of it. Her focus was on the heaping plate of food she was carrying. She plopped down on the lounge chair next to mine and settled in. Chloe shifted positions and stared intensely at Josie's plate.

"Sorry, Chloe," Josie said, reaching over to stroke her head. "This is people food."

Chloe barked once. She knew exactly what Josie was saying, but she didn't like what she was hearing.

Josie and I laughed. Chloe kept staring at the plate, but Josie was resolute. Chloe woofed one more time, but her heart wasn't in it. She was beaten, and she knew it.

"Chef Claire outdid herself," Josie said. "These barbecue shrimp are amazing. Did you try them?" She devoured another one, then caught the expression on my face. "Dumb question. Forget I even asked."

Josie momentarily forgot my deep and abiding commitment to avoid eating anything that comes from the water; either salt or fresh. But since she's in the process of working her way into an appetizer-induced coma, I'll forgive her temporary loss of memory.

"I know you must have gone to town on the cheesesteak sliders," she said, grabbing a deep-fried stuffed mushroom from her plate.

"Yes," I said, rubbing my stomach. "And the mushrooms, the Italian sausage and peppers, and the chicken-corn fritters."

"Did you try the bacon-wrapped figs stuffed with blue cheese?"

"Yeah," I said, holding my stomach. "I had a couple."

Josie raised an eyebrow at me as she chewed.

"Define a couple," she said.

"Eight. Maybe ten."

"Lightweight," she said, selecting another shrimp from her plate.

She held the plate out toward me. I shook my head and continued to rub my stomach.

"Okay," Josie said. "More for me."

Her ability to consume prodigious amounts of food without gaining a pound continued to baffle me. I'd made a solid effort today to keep up with her, but who was I kidding? If she hadn't decided to become a veterinarian, she would have had a bright future as a competitive eater.

"It's a nice turnout," Josie said. "John's gone above and beyond what anybody could expect."

"He certainly has," I said. "Have you seen him yet?"

"Only briefly," she said. "He seemed a bit distracted, but he's probably just trying to get everything wrapped up for the season."

"Yeah, I'm sure he is," I said, glancing down at Chloe who was focused on something on the other side of the lawn.

"But he did say he had a surprise for later on," Josie said, setting her empty plate on a nearby table.

"There's more?" I said.

"Apparently," she said, then stopped.

I heard her trying to swallow a gasp and followed her eyes to the other side of the lawn.

I recognized the man strolling our way along with a massive dog. They were both drawing a lot of attention and their progress toward us was slow.

"Who on earth is that?" Josie said, staring intensely at the man.

"That is the famous Summerman Lawless," I said, climbing out of the lounge chair. "And the dog is Murray."

"He's magnificent," Josie said.

"Are you referring to him or the dog?"

"What dog?" Josie asked.

I stared at her. It didn't happen very often. In fact, I'd only see it three times before. But there was no mistaking what I was witnessing. Josie's motor was running full throttle.

"You said he's famous?" she said, unable to take her eyes off the man who continued to make his way across the lawn.

"He's a musician originally from the area. Do you remember the band Life's Eclectic Nightmare?"

"LEN? Sure, I remember them. Aren't they the ones who died in a boating accident?"

"Everyone in the band except for one member. That's him," I said, waving to him.

"What's he doing here?" Josie said, clambering out of her lounge chair to stand next to me.

"He's got an island a couple of miles downriver. He tries to get to the River each summer, but I haven't seen him around this year."

"You know this man?" Josie asked, staring at me.

"Sure, I've known him for years," I said, shrugging. "He was ahead of me at school, but he's pretty tight with my mom. I had such a crush on him when I was younger."

"I'd be shocked if you hadn't," Josie said.

Murray spotted me and made a beeline for us. Chloe, completely unsure about what to do about the massive beast, barked, and then sat down near my feet and cocked her head. Murray stood on his back legs and gently placed his front paws on my shoulders.

"Hello, Murray," I said, vigorously rubbing his massive head.

Murray glanced down and spotted Chloe. They spent the next few minutes checking each other out, decided they liked each other and began playing and rolling in the grass.

"What a great dog," Josie said, apparently noticing the gigantic beast for the first time.

"Hi, Suzy. So good to see you."

"Hi, Summerman," I said, giving him a hug. "Where have you been all summer?"

"It's a long story," he said.

"All the good ones are," I said.

"Yeah, you're right. I spent most of the summer bouncing back and forth between Vegas and China."

"Well, I'm glad you made it here today," I said.

"John's making me sing for my supper," he said, laughing. "But for you and your rescue program, I'm happy to do it."

"You're going to play?" I said. "That's great."

I felt a small kick on my ankle and heard Josie's soft cough.

"Summerman, I'd like you to meet my best friend and business partner, Josie."

"Oh, yes. You're the vet I've heard so much about," he said, extending his hand. "It's nice to meet you."

"The pleasure is all mine," Josie said.

I glanced at the expression on her face and shook my head.

"Do I need to get the hose?" I whispered.

"I'm a *huge* fan," she said, ignoring me.

I grinned and glanced down at the lawn to hide it. Josie was gushing, and I made a mental note to remind her about it later. And the only thing that was *huge* around here at the moment, apart from Murray, was the lie she'd just told him. Josie spent about as much time listening to music as I did eating fish.

"Tell me about this magnificent animal," Josie said, kneeling to rub Murray's head. "A Newfie, Golden Retriever mix, right?"

"Very good. Most people don't get it on their first guess."

"Well, I'm a vet, so…"

"Interesting," Summerman said, studying Josie closely.

I'm sure he thought Josie was incredibly *interesting*, but he was playing it very cool. Josie was so used to deflecting the attentions of men she didn't find interesting, now that she was playing the role of pursuer and not getting the reaction she might have expected, she seemed unsure of herself. So for the moment Josie continued to focus on the dog.

When in doubt, play to your strengths.

"The woman who breeds them, calls them Goldenlands," Summerman said.

"I've never seen one," Josie said, putting Murray into a leg kicking trance as she scratched his stomach. "In fact, I've never even heard of the breed."

"Yeah, I'm not big on sharing them," he said, petting Chloe.

Josie, confused, stared at him. It was the first time any expression other than unbridled lust had crossed her face for several minutes.

"I own all of them," he continued.

"I don't understand," Josie said. "You own the entire breed?"

"The breeder is the only one I've found anywhere, so I pay her a lot of money to take care of all of them and keep them off the market. Except for the one that's currently under your spell," he said, laughing. "Consider yourself lucky, Murray. I'd need to have four legs to get one of those."

"Don't bet on it," I whispered, then flinched from the quick punch to my knee Josie delivered.

"Most rock stars collect things like houses and cars," he said. "I collect these guys. Weird, huh?"

"Maybe a little," I said. "But if you ever change your mind, I'll be more than happy to take a couple off your hands."

"I don't know if my breeder friend would appreciate that. She's pretty happy spending all day surrounded by unconditional love. But I'm sure I don't have to explain that to you guys."

"No," I said, nodding. "We get that one. Right, Josie?"

"Huh?" she said. "Oh, absolutely."

"Look, I need to run," Summerman said. "I need to do a quick sound check. But maybe I'll see you guys later."

"Absolutely," Josie said. "Maybe you could come over to the house for dinner sometime."

"I'd love too," he said. "But Murray and I are heading off tonight."

"Some people," I said, laughing. "The first day of fall arrives, and you're out of here like you got shot from a cannon."

"Well, Murray and I have a travel commitment we can't miss. Isn't that right, Murray?"

Murray woofed, and I swear he nodded his head.

"Okay," Summerman said. "I'll see you later. Suzy, great seeing you as always."

I moved in to accept his hug.

"Josie, it's been a pleasure meeting you," he said, extending his hand.

"Absolutely," she said, returning the handshake.

"You ready, Murray? Let's go see if we can find you a snack."

We returned his wave and watched them make their way back across the lawn. I snapped my fingers in front of Josie's face.

"Wow," she said, continuing to stare at them. "Is it my imagination or did I just make a complete fool of myself?"

"*Absolutely*," I said, laughing.

"Yeah, I was kind of repeating myself for a while there wasn't I?"

"*Absolutely*."

"Shut up," Josie said. Then she laughed and shook her head. "And to think I was beginning to wonder if my motor was still working."

"I'd say it's working fine," I said. "For a teenage girl anyway."

"Was I that bad?"

"*Absolutely* deplorable," I said, unable to stop laughing. "What do you have to say for yourself?"

"Woof."

Chapter 2

We strolled toward the section of lawn where a small stage had been set up. People were already sitting in folding chairs or on blankets spread out on the grass. Like us, everyone seemed a bit sluggish from the amount of food they'd eaten. Several people were even taking advantage of the temporary break in the festivities to catch a short nap.

A boat slowly approaching the main dock at the Yacht Club caught my attention. But calling it a boat was probably an insult. It was a magnificent yacht I estimated to be about seventy feet long. It was relatively short as far as yachts go, but it was sleek and cut through the water effortlessly. I nudged Josie and finally got her attention.

"Look at that," I said, unable to take my eyes off the craft.

"Geez, John said he had a new boat arriving today. I had no idea his company built anything like that."

"Is that Alice?" I said, staring at the young woman who was standing on the bow preparing to toss a line to John who was standing on the dock beaming at the yacht.

"It certainly is," Josie said. "I guess she decided not to go back to school after all."

Alice had spent the summer as an intern for Clay Bay's Chief of Police. But after dealing with the dead bodies of two murder victims, her interest in a criminology career had waned. I hadn't seen her since her internship ended and had just assumed she'd gone back to school for her junior year. She waved and tossed the bow line to John. Judging from the size of the smile on her face, it appeared she'd taken quite a shine to being on the water.

I guess spending time on a luxurious yacht has that effect on some people.

"It's amazing," Josie said. "How much do you think something like that costs?"

"Well," I said, staring at the yacht now tied to the dock. "It's not that long for a yacht, and it's not as tall as you might expect. But knowing John, I'm sure it's tricked out inside. I'll guess somewhere near five million, maybe ten."

"Geez," Josie whispered. "What a different life he leads, huh?"

"Yeah, but I'll stick with dogs," I said.

"Me too," she said, following me toward the dock.

John turned around when he heard our footsteps on the dock.

"What do you think, ladies?" he said, making a grand gesture at the yacht.

"It's incredible," I said.

It was all I had to offer. Fortunately, it was all I needed. It was one of the most amazing boats I'd ever seen.

"Did you build this one for yourself, John?" Josie asked.

"Oh, no," he said, laughing. "My tastes run much more pedestrian. We built it for a guy in Florida who wants to spend a year as a looper."

I nodded and looked up at the yacht.

Looper was the name for people who circumnavigated Eastern North America by water on a route known as the Great Loop. Loopers usually started their journey in Florida in the spring, headed north up the Intracoastal Waterway along the coasts of Georgia, South Carolina, and North Carolina, and continued from there to The Chesapeake Bay. From there the usual route was to continue to New York and up the Hudson River until reaching the Erie Canal. Traveling west along the Canal takes you to Lake Ontario where loopers can access the St. Lawrence if they desire to experience our beautiful area, particularly the Thousand Islands where we live. At some point in the fall, loopers make their way west across the Great Lakes to Chicago and then begin the southern leg along the Mississippi, and other waterways, before heading east and eventually ending up back in Florida. The total route exceeds 5,000 miles and takes months to complete, longer if the looper's trip includes extended breaks along the way.

"I thought the boats that traveled the Great Loop are a lot smaller than that one," I said.

"They are usually," John said, nodding. "That's what made the design of this one so much fun. It was a real challenge to make sure that it met the nautical requirements of the trip and still provided the luxury my client expects. If he's going to be spending the better part of a year on it, as he constantly reminds me, he's going to be comfortable doing it."

John laughed and continued to stare up at the yacht like a proud papa.

"What do you mean by the nautical requirements?" Josie asked.

"Well, there are only a couple of major ones," John said, turning to Josie. "Since it's an inland water route, we had to make sure our design incorporated the changing water levels in various parts of the route. The design had to ensure a maximum draft of not more than five feet."

"Draft is the amount of boat that's below the waterline, right?" Josie said.

"It is indeed," John said, nodding in approval. "Not bad for a landlubber, Josie."

Josie turned and made a face at me. It wasn't an attractive look.

"And you said I never pay attention," she said as her scrunchy face morphed into a wide grin.

Josie's prowess with boats and water was, to be kind, still evolving. It was understandable since she hadn't grown up around them. When she moved here to join me as co-owner of the Thousand Islands Doggy Inn, I thought I'd do her a favor by adopting the role of teacher when it came to all things nautical. It turns out I'm not the most patient of teachers and have a tendency to set unreasonably high expectations when it comes to learning and retention.

At least that's her opinion.

I think her progress has been slow because she sometimes has the attention span of a gnat.

But she'd gotten me this time.

"And I guess I'm not the lousy teacher you make me out to be," I said, glancing back up at the yacht. "I can't believe that thing doesn't draw more than five feet. That's impressive."

"Roger is an amazing engineer," John said. "I'd be lost without him." He turned back to Josie. "The other physical requirement is for the boat to have an overhead clearance of nineteen feet. And the boat needs to have a cruising range of at least five hundred miles. But given the size of the gas tanks on this baby, that won't be a problem."

"No problem until you see what it costs to fill them," I said, laughing.

"Yeah," John said. "But that's the least of my client's concerns."

"I kind of figured that one out," I said. "Must be nice. So, you're going to deliver the boat to him?"

"Well, not me personally," John said. "But my crew onboard is. Captain Bill, Roger, a couple of college kids I haven't met yet, and Alice will be setting off for Florida as soon as they're ready to go. It'll take them about a month. Maybe six weeks. I just need to make sure the thing performs as designed before I turn it over."

Alice climbed down the stairway and stepped onto the dock and headed our way. She smiled and waved and then gave all three of us a quick hug. She looked good; tanned and refreshed and I assumed relieved that there wasn't a dead body in sight.

"Is everything pretty much in order?" John asked her.

Alice shrugged and stared back at him.

"It's okay," she said. "But you need to have a word with Captain Hook and his first mate. They've been at each other's throats since we left Montreal."

"About what?" John asked.

"Who knows?" Alice said. "Maybe a bottle of rum for all I know. But this isn't what I signed up for, John. I can't listen to any more of that."

John frowned and rubbed his forehead.

"Those two," he said, placing a hand on Alice's shoulder. "Don't worry. I'll go have a chat with them to see what the problem is."

He walked down the dock and climbed aboard. I looked at Alice who was staring after him.

"So, no more school?" I said.

"No, not for a while," she said. "I thought I'd take the year off and do some traveling while I figured out what I want to do with my life."

"Good for you," Josie said. "You got lots of time."

"Would you mind telling my parents that?" Alice said, laughing. "They certainly aren't listening to me."

"They'll get over it," I said. "Besides, you'll learn a lot more about life over the next year than you would have in school."

"Yeah, I think that's what they're afraid of," Alice said, laughing. "I heard Chef Claire was doing the catering today."

"Yes, she is," I said.

"Great. I'm starved," Alice said. "How about we catch up over a plate of her food?"

Unconsciously, I rubbed my stomach and glanced at Josie who seemed to be giving the question serious consideration.

"I could eat," she said.

Chapter 3

Josie and I ate another plate of food while we chatted with Alice and I began to wonder if a food rehab program might be the next course of action for both of us. I sat on my chair, nodding at a story Alice was sharing about her recent trip to Montreal to pick up the yacht and resumed gently rubbing my stomach.

I knew I had to develop at least a modicum of restraint, but a trip through one of Chef Claire's buffet lines was an experience that needed repeating.

And if repetition was the key to perfecting a skill, I knew I must be approaching mastery.

Josie waved at Chef Claire, the mastermind behind today's feast. We'd met her a few months ago when she'd been the chef for a candy magnate at his island and then framed for his and his ex-wife's murder. But after we identified the actual killer, Chef Claire was released and had decided to stay in town until she determined where her next stop would be. Josie and I were currently doing a full court press to convince her to stay in Clay Bay. But Chef Claire was a warm weather girl, and the fall temperatures were continuing to drop. Despite our best efforts, I didn't like our chances of convincing her to stick around.

Right now, Chef Claire was carrying a tray filled with bowls and headed in our direction.

"Dessert?" Josie said, glancing at me.

I managed a brief shake of my head and small wave at Chef Claire.

"Hello, ladies," Chef Claire said. "How was your boat trip, Alice?"

"Life altering," she said, laughing. "And I saw just enough of that lifestyle to convince me I wanted it."

"Be careful what you wish for," Chef Claire said. "Would you like dessert?"

"Thanks," Alice said, reaching for one of the bowls.

"Josie?" Chef Claire said, holding the tray directly in front of Josie.

"Just don't get too close," I said, looking at the expression on Josie's face. If I didn't know better, I'd swear she hadn't eaten in a week. "On occasion, she's been known to bite her food servers by accident."

"Funny. And for the record, it was only that one time," Josie said, then focused on the tray in Chef Claire's hand. "What is it?"

"Let's see if you can tell me," Chef Claire said.

Josie selected a bowl and spoon and took a bite.

"Oh, my goodness," Josie said, savoring the dessert. "I think I need to sit down."

"What is it?" I asked, sneaking a peek inside the bowl.

"Let's see. It's a walnut and almond brownie with almond ice cream and a healthy splash of… Amaretto cream sauce over the top," Josie said.

"Very good," Chef Claire said, then extended the tray in my direction. "Suzy?"

"Not unless you're also handing out sweatpants," I said, unable to take my eyes off the tray.

Chef Claire laughed but stayed right where she was.

"You sure?" Chef Claire said, inching the tray even closer.

I folded like a cheap lawn chair and grabbed a bowl.

"I hate myself," I said through a mouthful. "What is wrong with me? I always thought I had a strong will."

"You do have a strong will. The problem is your incredibly weak won't," Josie said, grinning at Chef Claire and Alice.

I ignored their laughter and noticed John striding up the dock flanked by a man on either side. Their conversation was animated, and John was obviously not pleased by what he was hearing. I turned to Alice.

"That must be Captain Bill and Roger the engineer, right?" I said.

"That's them," Alice said, pausing briefly from her dessert to take a quick glance at the three men.

"It looks like they're still arguing," I said.

"Yeah, they've been going at it non-stop since we left Montreal," Alice said.

"About what?" I said.

"I'm not sure. Between all of Roger's engineering language and Captain's use of nautical terms, I was completely lost. I'm assuming it has something to do with the yacht, but I have no idea what it is. The boat seems perfect to me." Alice turned to Chef Claire. "Have you decided if you're going to accept John's offer?"

"I doubt it," Chef Claire said. "That's a lot of time to spend on a boat."

"What are you talking about?" I said, pausing mid-bite.

"John wants to hire Chef Claire to cook for us on our trip to Florida with the new yacht," Alice said.

"Actually, he made me a second offer," Chef Claire said, handing the dessert tray to one of the servers who headed off with it.

"Really?" Alice said, brushing the hair away from her face as she focused on Chef Claire.

"Yeah, just this morning," Chef Claire said. "He said that if I didn't want to make the Inland Waterway trip, I should just sign on to be his chef. Apparently, he's taking his personal boat down the St. Lawrence all the way to the Atlantic and then head south along the coast. He says he's going to meet you guys in Florida."

"I didn't know that," Alice said, glancing at John who was still in the middle of his conversation with Captain Bill and the engineer. "Are you going to take the job?"

"No, I don't think so," Chef Claire said. "I like John, but he's got quite the reputation as a player. I'm not sure I want to be out on the open water if he decides to try and get friendly."

Josie and I laughed. We'd both been the targets of John's affections in the past. We had successfully beaten them back and remained friends with him in the process, but then again we'd never been stuck on a boat with him.

"John would never force himself on anyone," Alice said.

"No, I'm not saying he would," Chef Claire said. "But who needs all that drama, right? And while I love the River, I'm not a big fan of being out on the ocean."

"That means you're going to stay in Clay Bay, right?" I said.

Chef Claire laughed.

"You guys are relentless," she said. "Right now, I'm considering sticking around until the first snowfall. I've never seen it snow before."

"Then you've come to the right place," Josie said.

The sound of a piano caught our attention.

"Showtime," Josie said, immediately striding off in the direction of the makeshift stage.

"Wow," Chef Claire said. "I don't think I've ever seen her move that fast. What got into her?"

"That would be Summerman," I said, strolling with Chef Claire toward the stage.

"I met him earlier," Chef Claire said. "For him, I'd stick around."

I nodded and kept walking as I watched Alice approach the three men who were still having an animated conversation. They kept talking when Alice approached, and John draped an arm around her shoulder, then slid his hand down until it reached her lower back. His hand seemed to linger there longer than I would have expected.

But I could easily have been wrong about that. Dessert had pushed me over the edge, and I could have been hallucinating from the onset of a food-induced coma.

Chapter 4

I stood waiting at the front of the stage for Josie who was standing next to Summerman on stage saying her goodbyes. He'd played for ninety minutes, electrified the crowd, apologized for his abrupt departure, and then quickly packed up and prepared to leave. At least he was trying to. Josie was doing her best to convince him to stay.

Jackson Frank, the Clay Bay Chief of Police, approached, trailed by his bulldog, Sluggo.

"Hey, Suzy," the Chief said. "Great show, huh?"

"Yeah, it was. Hey, Sluggo. Who's my boy?"

On cue, Sluggo rolled over and waited for his belly rub. I complied, and he was soon kicking his legs in the air as he squirmed on the grass. Chloe climbed on top of Sluggo and tried to assist me. Then she decided a belly rub of her own was in order. She stretched out next to Sluggo and rolled over. I used my free hand to comply with her demand.

It's a dog's world; fortunately, I get to live in it.

"I've lost my touch," Josie said, climbing down off the stage.

"Couldn't convince him to stay, huh?" I said, waving goodbye to Summerman who waited for the massive Murray to get settled into the front seat of his truck and then climbed in and drove off.

"No. And he said he wouldn't be back until next June," Josie said.

"Did he say where he's going?" I asked.

"Not really. He mentioned a couple of possible locations, but nothing specific. He's a little mysterious."

"You like that quality in your men, don't you?" I said, laughing.

"Yes, I do."

"I'll keep that in mind," Jackson said.

"You do that, Jackson," Josie said, grinning. "Hey, Sluggo."

Josie bent down and took over the belly rubbing duties. Sluggo's tongue dropped onto the lawn, and he snorted.

"You got your speech ready?" the Chief said.

"I think I'm all set," I said. "But I always get a bit nervous speaking in front of groups."

"Just use that old trick of picturing everyone in the audience in their underwear," the Chief said. "In case you're wondering, Josie, I'm wearing boxers."

"How about that?" Josie said, not even bothering to look up. "Me too."

I laughed at the look on the Chief's face. Either he was trying to figure out if Josie was joking, or he was trying to picture it in his mind. Either way, Josie's comment had shut him up. I stared out at the River and the ship that was making its way through the main shipping channel on its way to Lake Ontario about thirty miles away.

"Beautiful sunset," I said.

Josie stood and glanced out over the water. Then her eyes drifted back to the new yacht secured to the dock.

"What a boat," she said.

"John's been taking people on tours. Maybe he'll give us one later," the Chief said. "But I'd be happy just winning the one being raffled off. I bought twenty tickets."

We cringed at the sound of a microphone screeching with feedback. I turned and saw John standing next to a podium on the stage. He caught my eye and gestured for me to join him.

"That's my cue," I said, trying to hop up onto the stage. I failed miserably and then decided to use the three small steps located on the far side.

Josie snorted, and I glared at her.

"I'm just too full to make that jump," I said, defending my decision.

"I didn't say a word," she said, laughing.

I made my way to the far end then climbed onto the stage and approached John who was now sitting at a small table next to the podium.

"Having a good time?" he asked as he flipped through a small stack of note cards.

"Yeah, it's great, John," I said. "We can't thank you enough."

"It's the least I can do, Suzy," he said.

"I couldn't help but notice that you and the captain and engineer were having quite the discussion earlier," I said.

"Yeah," he said, shaking his head in disgust. "Those two geniuses made a mess of things. But I'll figure out a way to fix it."

"What did they do?" I asked.

"Apparently, one of them is a bit challenged by some pretty basic math," John said. "Which one I'm not sure yet so until I do know, I'm blaming both of them."

"I hear you asked Chef Claire to be your chef," I said.

"You're a wealth of information aren't you, Suzy?" he said, smiling but still giving me an odd look. "Have you been doing some snooping?"

"John, how long have you known me? When have I ever not been snooping?"

He laughed.

"Yes, I did ask Chef Claire. She's an amazing cook," he said, not looking up from his notes. "But she said no. She said she's not a fan of being out on the ocean, but I imagine she's worried that I'd hit on her."

"Would you?"

"Suzy, how long have you known me?" he said, finally glancing up at me.

I laughed.

"Touche. Dumb question. Forget I asked."

He went to the podium and asked the crowd to get settled. He waited until he had everyone's attention, then jumped right in.

"I'd like to thank all of you for coming today. It's been a great day, and I know that tonight will be even better. And for those of you who'd like to get a look at the inside of that magnificent craft sitting at the dock, I'm happy to give anyone interested a tour later on."

"I bet you are," a woman from the audience called out.

Laughter burst out, and John smiled and let the joke play itself out. As I said earlier, John has quite the well-established reputation.

"There goes your chance at a tour, Sally," John said, laughing. "And although he had to take off right after his performance, I'd like to thank Summerman for agreeing to play today."

Applause broke out, led by Josie's enthusiastic claps and whistles.

"And he played for free," John said. "I'm not even going to tell you how much money that saved me."

Another short burst of laughter broke out. Then John turned serious.

"Apart from being a day to say goodbye to summer and each other, today is about doing something for a very special program that Suzy and Josie run on behalf of dogs who need help. Their ongoing commitment to these rescue dogs and their unfailing commitment to a No Kill policy is commendable and needs our support. And it is my pleasure to present this check to them. Josie, please join us on stage so we can get some photos."

Thankfully, Josie didn't embarrass me by hopping up onto the stage. She climbed the stairs, and we stood on either side of John and posed for photos.

"And I have to thank all of you for supporting this year's raffle. We sold over one hundred and fifty thousand dollars in tickets, and local support was so strong that my company decided we would match, dollar for dollar, the total ticket sales. So it's my pleasure to present the owners of the Thousand Islands Doggy Inn with this check for three hundred and eight thousand dollars."

Everyone in the audience gasped, including Josie and me. We both hugged him and stared at the check. I felt tears sliding down my face, and I watched Josie brush back her own.

"John," I said. "This is too much."

"No, it's not," he said, touching my arm.

"You just fed and protected countless animals, John," Josie said.

"That's why we're here, right?" he said, gesturing for me to speak to the crowd.

I moved behind the podium and struggled for something to say. I glanced down at my note cards, then pushed them aside. I leaned forward toward the microphone and had just managed to get my mouth open when a blood-curdling scream erupted. It sounded like it came from the area near the dock.

I glanced at John and Josie who were both squinting through the darkness in the direction of the scream. I looked out at the crowd that had turned in their seats and craned their necks. The Chief, who'd been standing near the back with Sluggo, raced along the lawn with Sluggo valiantly chugging behind trying to keep up. He raced along the dock, clamored up the stairway that led onto the yacht and disappeared.

Josie and John raced in the direction of the screams. I scooped Chloe up in my arms, then handed her to a friend sitting in the front row and followed Josie and John. When we arrived at the dock, we heard another sound. This one was a combination of a howl and a throaty high-pitched squawk.

"What on earth is that?" John said, racing along the dock.

"That's Sluggo," I said, running as fast as my legs would carry me.

In case you're wondering, it wasn't very fast. I blamed my last trip through the buffet line.

"It certainly is," Josie said, racing past both of us like we were standing still. "And he's in trouble."

Josie climbed the stairway with John following close behind. I eventually reached the stairway and gasped and wheezed as I completed the short climb. I found Josie below deck in what I assumed was the master stateroom of the yacht. Spread across the bed was Roger the Engineer, his head bent at an odd angle, and a vacant stare plastered on his face. On the floor nearby, the Chief was lying in a pool of blood that was oozing from a wound on the back of his head. Sluggo continued his distress cry as he nudged the Chief with his head and paws. Josie bent down and picked Sluggo up. He kicked at her and snapped his jaws, then realized who was holding him and calmed down a bit. But he continued staring down at the Chief and whimpering softly.

The partygoers began arriving but stayed back from the scene. Others craned their necks around tight corners or through the windows that ran alongside the upper deck of the yacht. I caught a glimpse of Alice and Chef Claire in the crowd, but my eyes kept returning to my gravely injured friend.

The whole scene was a surreal kaleidoscope displaying an alternate reality, and it broke my heart. I knelt down to see if there was anything I could do to help Jackson, who seemed to be unconscious. John was already on the phone requesting an ambulance.

Chloe seemed to appear out of nowhere at my feet, and I reached down to pick her up. I held her tight and heard the sound of an ambulance getting louder by the second.

Chapter 5

When the ambulance arrived, the decision was quickly made to transport Jackson to the Upstate Medical Center for emergency surgery. The medical staff wheeled our unconscious friend who was strapped tight to a stretcher down the dock and then into the back of the ambulance. It roared off to begin the one hour journey with its siren blaring.

My legs trembled as I made my way down the stairway back onto the dock. Josie was already there holding Sluggo who continued his heartbreaking cries and whimpers. I set Chloe down, and she looked up at Sluggo, then back at me. She barked once, but like the rest of us seemed to feel helpless.

"Should we stick around and see if the police want to talk to us?" I said.

Josie thought about my question, then Sluggo whimpered again.

"Let's get out of here," Josie said. "They know where to find us."

I nodded and noticed the amount of blood that was smeared all over her and Sluggo. Dazed, we headed for my SUV, waving half-heartedly to other partygoers who were as shocked as we were. I drove slowly, and when we arrived at the Inn, we headed straight for the bathing room and began the task of washing Sluggo. Josie was going through the motions like a zombie.

"I've got this," I said to Josie. "Why don't you take Chloe up to the house and then take a shower? You're covered in blood."

"Yeah," Josie said, staring off into the distance.

"Are you going to be okay?" I said.

"I'll be fine," she said. "It's Jackson I'm worried about."

I nodded. I shared the same sentiment.

"Who was the dead guy?" Josie whispered.

"That was Roger. The engineer."

"Who would want to kill him?" she said.

"I don't know," I said. "But who would want to hurt Jackson? It doesn't make any sense."

"No, it doesn't," Josie said, finally managing to look at me.

Josie gave me a small wave and exited the bathing room and whistled for Chloe to follow her. Chloe remained sitting and cocked her head at me.

"Go with Josie, girl," I said, rubbing her head.

I watched Chloe trot off to join Josie and turned my attention to Sluggo. Despite our best efforts to comfort him, he continued to emit the strange wail that I was sure was going to haunt my dreams. I rinsed the last of the red-tinged shampoo off him, then sat down on the tile floor and held him tight. He continued to tremble and softly howl and wail. More than anything I wanted to make him feel better, to erase whatever images from the boat were rolling through his head, and make him whole again.

I unfolded a large towel and wiped him dry. At this point in his bathing ritual, Sluggo would always try to grab the towel and play a game of tuggy with the person giving him his bath. But not tonight. Sluggo stood still with a vacant expression, and his chest heaved as he continuing whimpering.

I continued to sit on the tile floor hugging him. Eventually, he stretched out and tucked his head under my arm. We remained in that position until Josie arrived a half hour later carrying two large mugs of coffee. She was dressed in sweats and had a towel draped over her shoulders. I gently moved Sluggo aside and climbed to my feet. I took a sip of coffee as I stared down at the distressed bulldog.

"How's he doing?" Josie asked, kneeling down to pet him.

"Not good," I said. "Worse than us I think. And that's pretty bad."

Josie walked to the other side of the room and unlocked a cabinet. Moments later she returned holding a small pill. She leaned down, gently forced Sluggo's mouth open and worked the pill down his throat. She rubbed his head and climbed to her feet.

"I gave him an Acepromazine," she said. "That should calm him down. Hopefully, he'll sleep. But let's get him up to the house. He can stay with me in my room."

"We need to call Jackson's mom and dad," I said.

"They called while I was up at the house," Josie said. "They're already heading to the hospital. They said they'd call back as soon as Jackson comes out of surgery."

"Brain surgery?"

"Yeah," Josie said.

I managed a nod as I headed for the door. Sluggo apparently didn't want to be alone, and he came to me without being called. We made our way out of the Inn and climbed the stairs that led to the house. Chef Claire greeted us in the kitchen, and Josie led Sluggo to her room.

"How's Sluggo doing?" Chef Claire said.

"About the same as the rest of us I'm afraid," I said.

Chef Claire shook her head.

"What is it?" I asked.

"For such a small town, there sure seems to be a lot of nasty business around."

"I think we're just going through a rough patch," I said.

But Chef Claire had a point. In the few months she'd been here, her former boss and his ex-wife were murdered. And his girlfriend had come within an inch of losing her life. And tonight, one more person had been killed while another, one of our best friends, was barely hanging on. I choked back an overload of emotions and sat down. Josie entered the kitchen and sat down across from me.

"Sluggo's on my bed, and Chloe offered to babysit," Josie said. "The two of them are snuggled in for the night I think."

"Is there going to be any room for you?" I said, managing a chuckle.

"Oh, I'm not even going to bother fighting for bed space with those two. I'm just going to sleep on the couch," she said, laughing.

"Since it looks like we're going to be up for a while, how about I make a snack?" Chef Claire said.

I considered the offer, thought about how much food I'd consumed during the day, and shook my head. I glanced at Josie and realized she was giving it serious consideration.

"What were you thinking about making?" Josie said.

"I thought I'd whip up a quick batch of the bacon wrapped chilidogs," Chef Claire said.

I was sure that nothing could bring me out of the funk I was in at the moment, but if anything had the smallest glimmer of hope, it was a couple of Chef Claire's chilidogs.

"I guess I could eat," I said, hating myself for even thinking it, much less saying it out loud.

Chef Claire began rummaging through the fridge, and I poured wine for all of us. I checked my phone for messages for the third time in fifteen minutes, rubbed my forehead, and then heard the car roaring up the driveway. I glanced out the window at the black Mercedes.

"Here comes the floorshow," I said, watching my mother make her way toward the house.

I opened the kitchen door, and my mother gave me a quick peck on the cheek as she stepped inside.

"Hello, darling," she said. "Any news?"

"Hi, Mom," I said. "No, we think he's still in surgery."

"Good evening, ladies," she said smiling at Josie and Chef Claire. Then she realized what was happening. "Darling, I watched both of you work your way through the buffet line at least three times. How could you even think about eating?"

"Bacon wrapped chilidogs," Josie said.

"Oooh," my mother said. "Well, maybe I'll just have a little bite of yours."

"I don't like your chances, Mrs. C.," Josie said, laughing.

"What happened to the Porsche, Mom?" I said.

My standing joke is that my mother changes cars more often than most people change their socks. But considering the way she was going through them the past few months, maybe it wasn't the joke I made it out to be.

"It wasn't the most comfortable of rides," she said, pouring herself a glass of wine. "The suspension was very rigid, and I could feel every bump in the road."

"I wouldn't have thought that you'd feel any bumps since you always seem to be airborne every time I see you on the road."

"Funny, darling," she said as she watched Chef Claire work her magic in the kitchen.

My mother loves to drive fast; way too fast. I'm not joking about that. In fact, it's one of the things we argue about on a regular basis. But since she used to be the mayor of Clay Bay and is still on the town council, most of the local authorities tend to let her off with a warning. And when it comes to her driving habits, I think a short stay in jail might do her a world of good, but I doubt that will ever come to pass. She has a ton of money, is on a first name basis with every judge and lawyer within a hundred mile radius, and I know for a fact she wouldn't be caught dead wearing orange.

My phone buzzed, and I recognized the number.

"Hi, Mr. Frank," I said.

I realized everyone else in the kitchen had stopped what they were doing to listen, so I set the phone on the table and put it on speaker.

"Hi, Suzy," the Chief's father said. He sounded worn out.

"I've got you on speaker, Mr. Frank. I'm here with my mom, Josie, and Chef Claire. What's the news?"

"Not much yet," he said. "But they're already talking about maybe having to do a second surgery."

"What?" I whispered.

"There's still some severe swelling and a bit of blood leaking. The doctors aren't quite sure where it's coming from."

"Has he been able to talk yet?" I said.

"No, he was unconscious, and now he's heavily sedated. We should know more in the morning."

"Do you need anything?" my mother said.

"No, I think we're good. Thanks. Look, I need to run. I'll let you know as soon as we hear anything."

He ended the call, and the four of us stared at each other.

"Jackson's a tough guy," Josie said. "He'll hang in there."

Desperate to believe her, I nodded and glanced up at the ceiling and said a silent prayer.

Chapter 6

It wasn't until around ten the next morning when Josie and I discovered we couldn't find the check for $308,000. And since we'd learned fifteen minutes earlier that Jackson was still in critical condition and scheduled for another surgery that afternoon, the loss of the check paled by comparison to the grave condition of our friend.

But I'd be lying if I said it didn't get our attention.

Josie called John at his office, and we were relieved when he told her that he had the check. We checked in on activities at the Inn, made sure Sluggo and Chloe were settled in at the house with Chef Claire, and then drove into town.

There was a flurry of police activity happening on and around the yacht and yellow crime tape sealed the investigation area off from the general public and snoops like Josie and me. We were escorted into John's office and sat down and waited for him to finish a phone call.

"What a mess," he said, hanging up.

"It's quite a scene out there," I said.

"And it looks like it's going to stay that way for a couple of days," he said, reaching into his desk drawer. He slid a sealed envelope across the desk. "I believe this is yours."

Josie opened the envelope, and again the number on the check took my breath away. Josie slid the envelope into her bag, brushed her hair back from her face, and draped one leg over the other. John didn't miss a single movement.

Even in times of grief, I guess players keep doing what they do.

But the man had just raised over three hundred thousand dollars for our dog rescue program, so I decided to forgive him for a few seconds of unrequited lust. I'm not even sure Josie noticed.

"Won't a couple of days put a crimp in your plans to get the yacht to Florida?" I said.

"Not really," he said. "As long as it doesn't remain a crime scene too long. But I do need to get a crew in there."

"To clean up, right?" I said.

"That's part of it," John said. "But that'll be a piece of cake."

At the mention of the word cake, Josie's ears perked up, and I knew a stop at Patterson's bakery on our way home had just been added to our itinerary.

"I need to get a crew in there to do some remodeling," he said.

"What?" I said, baffled. "John, the boat is brand new, and it's gorgeous."

"Yes, it is," he said with a shrug. "But one thing you constantly face dealing with clients, especially rich ones like the guy in Florida, is their unpredictability. He took a look at the final photos we sent him and decided he wanted to make some changes."

"To what?" I said.

I could understand maybe swapping out the mattress given the fact that Roger the Engineer had met his demise on it last night, but making any other changes seemed almost sacrilegious.

"He wants to change the décor inside. At first, he couldn't wait to see the combination of marble and Black Ironwood."

"Black Ironwood?" Josie said, raising an eyebrow.

"It's very rare and very expensive," John said. "He just had to have it. Now he can't wait to get rid of it. So we need to swap it and all the marble out for some crappy synthetic material he's been reading about."

"How long is that going to take?" I said.

"With the right crew, maybe a week. Two tops. With the wrong crew, probably a month. And I don't have a month. The guy wants his new boat."

"You'd think he might have some patience since he's the one who's creating the delay," I said.

"Yeah, that's what I told him," John snapped. Then he softened immediately. "Sorry, I'm not taking it out on you. It's just that with what happened to Roger and the Chief last night I'm on the razor's edge. You know what I mean."

Josie and I both nodded.

"Do the police have any idea who did it?" I said.

"Not yet," he said. "They're still interviewing all the guests from last night. And you can expect a call from them at some point."

Again, we both nodded.

"The scream we heard was from a woman," I said.

"Yeah," John said. "But the police don't necessarily think it was a woman who did it."

"Do they think the person who killed the engineer was also the one who attacked Jackson?" Josie said.

"I think that's their working theory for now. The assumption is that the Chief just happened to show up in the wrong place at the wrong time. And maybe the killer heard him coming and then surprised him from behind."

"What did Jackson get hit with?" I said, realizing that I hadn't seen any weapon on the floor.

"It was a wrench used to work on boat engines. It had gotten kicked or tossed into a corner. One of the cops found it last night."

We heard a soft knock on the door.

"Come in," John said.

Alice, looking very much the worse for wear, entered and stood in front of the desk.

"Sorry to interrupt, John," she said. "But the police have a few more questions for you."

"Of course they do," he said, rising out of his chair. "Ladies, I hope your day improves. And if you hear anything about Jackson, please let me know."

"Will do, John," I said. "And thanks again for all you did for us."

"Don't mention it," he said with a quick wave, then departed.

Alice sat down between us and fiddled with her hands.

"Are you okay?" Josie said.

"No. What? Who me? Yeah, I'll be fine," Alice said, transitioning to full-on handwringing. "It's just a lot to handle. If anything happened to Jackson, I don't know what I'd do. I mean, obviously, something has already happened, but if he doesn't come out of it okay… well, you know what I mean, right?"

"Yes, we do," I said.

Then the waterworks arrived, and tears streamed down Alice's face. My eyes also welled up, and I saw Josie wipe the side of her face with the back of her hand. We did our best to comfort Alice and eventually she stopped crying. She exhaled loudly, wiped her eyes dry, and then blew her nose.

"I can't wait to get out of here," she said, shaking her head. "Florida sounds pretty good at the moment."

"What are you going to do once you get there?" I said.

"I'm sure I'll think of something," she said, shrugging.

Chapter 7

Josie and I had met Detective Joe Abrams during the summer when he was investigating the murder of the candy magnate and his ex-wife. He was a no-nonsense cop who asked good questions, listened closely to your responses, and judging by the speed his pen was moving across the page, took excellent notes.

Although I'd never really thought about it before I imagined the ability to take good notes was an important part of the job. As I watched him nod and furiously scribble into his notebook, I knew that if I tried to listen and write that fast, I wouldn't be able to read a word later. Or remember anything I was told.

I wondered if he always trusted himself to write in ink.

I wondered if he might have minored in journalism in college.

I wondered if cops ever learned how to take shorthand.

I wondered if my answers to his questions were coming out as jumbled as my current thoughts.

I was a mess and needed to get an update on Jackson's condition soon, or I was going to lose it. We were told he was going in for a second surgery where the doctors would be trying to relieve some of the pressure on his brain.

At the moment, Detective Abrams was sitting with Josie, Chef Claire, and me at our kitchen table drinking coffee. Sluggo was laying at Josie's feet, breathing heavily and occasionally emitting the heartbreaking whimper we'd been hearing since the incident on the boat. Chloe was under the table with her head propped up on her two front paws keeping a close eye on Sluggo.

"Is he going to be okay?" Detective Abrams said, glancing down at Sluggo.

"Eventually, yes," Josie said, stroking Sluggo's head. "He's just been traumatized."

Detective Abrams furiously scribbled a note.

I couldn't contain myself any longer.

"Was that really worth writing down?" I snapped.

Josie and Chef Claire stared at me like I'd lost my mind.

"I beg your pardon," Detective Abrams said, glancing up at me.

"Josie's last response didn't sound very newsworthy. Can I ask you what you just wrote down?"

He stared at me, then read from the page.

"Sluggo. Bulldog. Traumatized since the attack. Pick up dog food. Remind Sue about tomorrow's vet appointment."

He looked up and forced a small smile in my direction.

"Happy?" he said.

I felt my face turn red.

"You're conducting an interview and working on your to-do list at the same time?" I said.

I had no idea why I felt the need to double down and poke a verbal stick at a cop.

But in my defense, like I said earlier, I'm a total mess at the moment.

"What can I say?" Detective Abrams said. "I'm a multitasker."

"Hey, wait a minute," Josie said, snapping her fingers. "Sue Abrams is your wife? I knew the name sounded familiar, but I didn't make the connection."

"Twenty-five years next month," he said, beaming with pride.

"Why does that name ring a bell?" I said.

"Wally. The basset hound," Josie said, laughing.

"Oh, I love Wally," I said.

"Everybody loves Wally," he said, smiling.

"We've met at least three times in the past, Detective Abrams. Why didn't you ever bother to tell us Wally was your dog?"

"It was probably because I was always investigating a murder," he said.

He let his response hang in the air. Defeated, I tucked my verbal stick back in my mouth.

"I guess you've got a point," I whispered.

Josie snorted.

She has a tendency to do that whenever I make a fool of myself in public. I don't think it's one of her better qualities, but as my best friend in the world she can get away with it. Besides, I wasn't in a position to make an issue of it at the moment.

"So, let's go through this one more time," Detective Abrams said, transitioning from proud dog owner back into a cop. "We've confirmed that the two of you were on stage with John accepting the check when everyone heard the scream coming from the boat. And Chef Claire, you were behind the stage with the rest of the catering crew doing cleanup."

All three of us nodded.

"And none of you saw or heard anything before the scream that indicated something might be amiss?" he said, pen poised at the ready.

I wondered if he was expecting to hear an important piece of information that might help him crack the case or if he'd just remembered he needed to pick up milk on his way home.

I kicked myself under the table and checked my phone for new messages.

"No, I didn't," Chef Claire said.

Josie shook her head.

I flashed back to the conversation I'd seen John having with Captain Bill and the dead engineer, but I kept my mouth shut and shook my head.

I wondered if perhaps I should have mentioned it.

I wondered if John or Captain Bill had mentioned the conversation to Detective Abrams.

I wondered if they hadn't bothered to share that piece of information, why not?

I wondered how I could find out.

"So, Detective Abrams, do you have a list of suspects yet?" I said.

"Sure. After I cross the three of you off the list, I'll be down to about a hundred and fifty," he said, laughing.

Every time I thought I'd come up with a reason not to like this guy, he took the air out of my balloon. He was a good man doing an incredibly difficult job and obviously very proud of the fact that he was about to celebrate his silver wedding anniversary. And he was a dog lover.

I wondered what on earth was wrong with me.

But I chalked it up to the current situation with Jackson and the fact that I was a complete mess.

I think I may have mentioned that.

He thanked us for our time and departed, pausing to reach down and pet Sluggo and Chloe before heading out the kitchen door. Chef Claire followed him out to head into town to do the grocery shopping. Josie and I decided to take Sluggo and Chloe for a walk. At first, Sluggo was reluctant to get up off the kitchen floor, but he seemed to perk up when the fresh air hit him. Chloe didn't need any convincing, and she bounded down the steps and sat waiting for us slowpokes at the edge of the lawn.

"You've got that look," Josie said. "I've been wondering when it would show up."

"What look?" I said.

"You know exactly what look I'm talking about," she said. "It's your *I need to solve a mystery look*."

"Yeah, I guess," I said, glancing out at the River and fall foliage. Even seeing that gorgeous sight didn't improve my mood. "But this is different. This one is personal."

"Yes, it is," Josie said, nodding.

"So where do we start?" I said, tossing a tennis ball for Chloe.

"Probably the way we always do," she said, laughing. "You know, muddle around and see what shakes out."

"You heard Detective Abrams. Anyone at the party could have done it. And maybe it was someone else altogether who wasn't there."

"Why didn't you mention the conversation you saw John having with the captain and engineer?"

"I'm not exactly sure," I said. "Why didn't you?"

"I think I wanted first to find out if John had told the police about it."

"I thought the same thing," I said.

"And I think it's possible that I was afraid to find out that John might somehow be involved," Josie said.

"You don't think he could have killed that man and then done that to Jackson, do you?"

"No, of course not," she said. "But it's possible that John does know who might have done it. And if that conversation has something to do with it, and if John didn't tell the police about it, that would tell us a lot."

"It would, wouldn't it?" I said.

"I wonder if it would be possible to find out a bit more about this Captain Bill?" I said, glancing over at her as we continued to stroll across the lawn and past the flower beds that had looked fantastic only a few short weeks ago but had now given up the fight.

"Yeah," Josie said. "Something about him bothers me."

"And Alice said he and Roger the Engineer had been fighting the whole time on the way back from Montreal."

"And then John made that comment about how those two *geniuses* were somehow math challenged. What on earth did he mean by that?"

"I have no idea," Josie said, grabbing a Snickers bar from her coat pocket. "I imagine that building a yacht like that from scratch involves all sorts of math."

"And who is this mysterious owner in Florida? At the last minute, he decides to remodel the inside of the boat? Who does something like that?" I said, feeling the adrenaline start to flow.

"The rich and finicky," Josie said, laughing. "I thought you'd recognize that one right away."

"Leave my mother out of it," I said, laughing along. "You know what we need to do, don't you?"

I came to a stop and whistled for Chloe.

"Head back to the house and see what Chef Claire is making for dinner," Josie said, swallowing the last bite of her Snickers.

"Well, sure, that goes without saying," I said, kneeling down to greet Chloe. "Good girl."

"And the other thing we need to do is ask John what he plans to do with all the granite and Black Ironwood he's ripping out of the boat. Maybe he'll sell it to us cheap. Imagine how good that would look in the kitchen."

I nodded. And that thought had already crossed my mind. It would look fantastic.

"We can ask him," I said. "And that would give us the perfect excuse to swing by his office and take another look around. I would love to get a good look at that boat. I'm betting it's somehow at the center of this thing. That is unless Roger the Engineer got caught doing something he shouldn't have," I said, trying to sort through all the questions rolling around my head.

"You mean like sleeping with the wrong person?" Josie said.

"It has been known to happen," I said.

"Not to us," Josie said, laughing.

"Well, there's always the possibility of hooking up with Summerman next summer, right?"

"A lot of good that's going to do me in February," Josie said.

I laughed so hard it startled Chloe. Even Sluggo looked up at me.

"But I think you might be right," I said. "We need to get a closer look at that boat."

"As long as it's still a crime scene, we'll never get anywhere near it," Josie said, removing another Snickers from her pocket.

"Maybe not during the day," I said, then noticed the candy bar. "Really? You're going to spoil your appetite."

Then I caught the blank stare she was giving me, and I shook my head.

"Never mind. For a moment, I forgot who I was talking to."

And for the record, Chef Claire made a lobster mac and cheese that made our knees buckle.

Josie, showing remarkable restraint, stopped at two servings. I'd made a silent vow to keep up with her and managed a tie. I probably could have forced down a third, but needed to save room for dessert.

Chocolate-pistachio cannoli.

Yeah, I know. Not bad for a Monday night dinner at home.

And Chef Claire even made her own ricotta.

I struggle just trying to get the store bought version out of the packaging.

Final cannoli score: Josie, the Bottomless Pit, 5; Suzy, the Gluttonous Wonder, 2.

Chapter 8

By the time I'd finished taking a short nap after dinner and regained the ability to walk upright without groaning, it was almost midnight. I pulled on a pair of black sweatpants and a black sweater. I pinned my hair up and completed the outfit with a black wool ski hat I'd bought to wear whenever I went cross skiing in the winter. In all honesty, this was the first time I'd worn it since I tried it on at the store three years ago.

I said I'd bought it to wear *when* I went. Maybe I should rephrase that to *if* I went. It's been quite a while since I've made it out the door to trek through snowy woods with two long, narrow pieces of fiberglass strapped to my feet carrying poles that could poke an eye out. And the last time I'd gone cross country skiing, an old boyfriend laughingly remarked that I looked like a flamingo trying to twerk.

We stopped dating soon after that.

But the hat looked great on me.

I headed for the living room and found Josie waiting for me. She was resplendent in a black track suit and lounging on the couch with Sluggo on one side and Chloe on the other. They were both sleeping, and Sluggo was snoring. I took that as a good sign although he still wasn't eating. Josie glanced over her shoulder when she heard me come in.

"Nice hat," she said.

"Thanks," I said, then stopped when I saw what was in her hand. I shook my head and stared in disbelief at the cannoli. "Really?"

"What can I say? Unlawful entry always makes me hungry," she said. "And it might be awhile before I get another shot at these. I doubt whatever jail we land in will have them on the menu."

"We are not going to jail," I said.

"Hmmm. If you say so," Josie said, polishing off the last of the cannoli and getting up off the couch.

"Do you think the dogs will be okay by themselves?" I said, stroking Chloe's head.

"Chef Claire got back about an hour ago and said she'd keep an eye on them," Josie said, heading for the kitchen door. "All right. Let's get this over with."

We made the short drive into town and parked on the street a safe distance from the yacht. By safe, I mean far enough away to have plausible deniability should someone ever start asking questions.

Fortunately, there was no moon, and it was very dark except for a solitary light at the top of a pole near the entrance to the dock.

"Maybe we should have come in by boat," Josie said, glancing up at the light.

"Maybe," I said. "But once we get away from that light, we should be okay."

"Yeah, I'm sure we'll be just fine," Josie said. "Why on earth did I agree to this?"

"Shhh. Not so loud," I whispered. "And we're doing this for Jackson, remember?"

"Okay," she whispered. "Let's just get it done. I'm freezing."

I nodded. So was I. Although it was only late September, summer was long gone, and it wouldn't be long before we had our first frost. If the temperature kept dropping, it could even happen tonight.

We casually strolled past the light, then ducked under the yellow tape strung across the front of the dock. We tiptoed our way through the darkness, and soon we were standing in front of the stairway that led up to the yacht.

"I guess that wasn't so hard," I said, already breathing heavily.

"You really need to get to the gym, Suzy," Josie said, chuckling softly.

I bent at the waist and put my hands on my knees and managed to nod my head in agreement. I stood up and pointed at the stairway.

"Wait," Josie said. "What's our cover story in case anybody sees us?"

"I thought we went over that in the car," I said, shaking my head.

"No, I don't think we did," Josie said.

I thought back to our car ride and realized I'd had the cover story conversation with myself. I really need to stop doing that.

"Sorry about that. My mistake. If anybody asks, we were out for a late night jog, and we thought we heard a sound coming from the boat."

Josie tried to stifle her laugh, but it escaped and echoed across the water.

"Us? Out for a late night jog?"

"Shhh," I whispered. "You got anything better?"

"No," she said, still chuckling under her breath.

"And no one is going to see us," I whispered. "The boat has to be empty, and people usually don't just happen to show up at an official crime scene in the middle of the night."

"We're here," Josie said.

"Yes," I whispered. "And that's what gives us the element of surprise."

"Unbelievable," Josie said as she reached for the railing on the side of the stairway and began the short climb.

Laboring, I followed her up, and soon we were both standing on the deck of the yacht. At least I think it must have been the deck. I couldn't see my hand in front of my face.

"Dark," I whispered.

"Brilliant deduction, Sherlock."

"Don't start snarking at me," I whispered.

"This is the stupidest thing I've ever let you talk me into," Josie whispered.

"Oh, I can think of a lot stupider."

"Stupider? Is that even a word?" she said.

"Of course it's a word," I said.

"C'mon, let's get going. I'm freezing my butt off."

"Okay, okay," I said, trying to compose my thoughts. "I'd like to take a look below deck."

"Good idea," Josie whispered. "It's probably a lot warmer down there."

I slowly felt my way across the deck until I reached the door that led below deck. I grabbed the handle and then turned back to Josie.

"It's locked," I whispered.

"Really? Now why on earth would anybody bother to lock that door? I mean, this thing is only worth millions."

"You're getting snarky again," I snapped.

"Shhhh," Josie whispered. "You're lucky I'm not throwing you overboard."

I shuddered at the thought of swimming in the St. Lawrence at this time of year. The water temperature wouldn't kill you the way it would if you fell in during the winter, but it would certainly get your attention.

I tried the handle one more time. I wasn't surprised it was still locked, but I think it's important to recheck your facts.

"You think we should try to figure out a way to get it open?" I whispered.

"Sure," Josie whispered. "Let's see if we can find a way to turn a simple misdemeanor into a felony."

"You are not being very helpful," I said.

"I think we're just going to have to agree to disagree on that," Josie whispered. "If I wasn't here, you would have already busted a window and climbed in."

"Maybe," I whispered, then cocked my head. "Did you hear that?"

"I certainly did," Josie whispered as she took a step back. "There's somebody in there."

I held an ear against the door and tried to hear what was happening below deck. Moments later, I pulled my head away and looked at Josie.

"There are two people down there. A man and a woman," I said.

"What are they doing?"

"Well, they sure aren't sleeping," I said.

"What? Oh, I get it. Not sleeping," Josie said.

"Why would they feel the need to come here?" I said, stepping back from the door.

"Maybe for the gentle rocking of the boat or the luxurious surroundings, but I'm going to guess it's because they don't want anybody to know."

"That makes sense," I said. "But they'd have to have a key, right?"

"Yeah," Josie said. "Maybe we can ask John who has one."

"Good idea," I said, then stopped. "But what if it's John who's down there?"

"Why would John be down there? You've seen his place. It's remote and very secure. Not to mention luxurious."

I couldn't disagree with Josie's logic. We'd been to John's house several times for parties over the years. If he wanted to keep an affair secret, his house was the perfect place to do it. Before I had time to consider other possibilities, a light below deck came on. Josie and I panicked and made a dash toward the starboard side and ducked down near the railing.

"This is bad," Josie whispered.

"Yeah, definitely not one of our better moments," I whispered.

"Nice job with this one, Columbo," she said.

"Shhh," I said peering toward the door.

The door opened, and we saw the silhouette of a man holding a long object.

"What's that in his hand?" I whispered. "A pool cue?"

"No," Josie whispered. "It's not a pool cue."

"Baseball bat?"

"No. I think it might be-"

She was interrupted by the unmistakable sound of a shell being racked into a pump action shotgun. Hearing that sound on a TV show or in a movie always got my attention. But hearing it knowing that you were the intended victim was terrifying. I grabbed Josie's hand and squeezed it hard.

"What are we going to do?" I whispered.

"We're going to get out of here," she whispered, her teeth chattering.

"Are you shivering out of fear or the cold?" I said.

"Oh, I'm sure it's a lot of both," she said. "He's blocking our way. We'll never make it back to the stairway."

In the darkness, I heard soft footsteps slowly heading in our direction.

"You know what we're going to have to do, right?" I whispered.

"Yes," she whispered, slowly rising to her feet. "And I can't begin to tell you how much I hate you at the moment."

"This is so going to suck," I said, standing up. I grabbed Josie's arm and pointed it in the direction we needed to head. "About twenty feet ahead."

"Yeah, I see it," she said, snatching her arm away.

And then we both started running along the deck until we reached a sitting area that extended out from the railing. I imagine it would be the perfect spot to do some sunbathing while enjoying a relaxing trip to the Caribbean. But right now it would have to suffice as a diving board. I jumped up onto the sitting area and landed with both feet, then launched myself up and over the side of the boat and fell through the cold night air until I splashed a few seconds later into the freezing water of the St. Lawrence River.

My feet touched the muddy bottom of the shallow water, and I surfaced, stifling my scream from the shock of the cold water by biting down on my forearm. I located Josie treading water next to me gasping for breath. She tugged my arm and pointed at the boat. We swam underwater for about ten feet and then popped to the surface and held onto the side of the boat.

"I doubt if he can see us under here," I finally managed to stammer.

"You are so gonna pay for this," Josie whispered. "This water is freezing."

"Look on the bright side," I whispered. "At least it's not February."

"Suzy, I swear, if it weren't for the fact that you're about to die of hypothermia, I'd kill you."

"Relax," I said. "We need to figure out a way to get out of the water without being seen."

"Or getting shot," she said.

"Yeah, good point," I said, beginning to feel the weight of my clothes trying to pull me down.

Josie glanced around at the dimly lit shoreline that was about a hundred feet away.

"I don't like our chances," she said. "Maybe we can slip around to the other side of the boat and hide under the dock."

"Yuk," I said. "Can you imagine what might be lurking under that dock?"

"Well not until now I wasn't," she snapped.

"Shhh," I said. "Do you hear that?"

"I do," Josie said, paddling forward for a better look at the dock. "They're leaving. And they're definitely in a hurry."

"Can you see who it is?"

"No, but they just reached the end of the dock and headed off in different directions."

We waited for the sound of cars starting, but heard nothing. Another two minutes passed before we made our way around the boat and used the bottom rung of the stairway to pull ourselves up out of the water and onto the dock. I stayed on all fours and tried to catch my breath, but the cold was relentless. Josie helped me to my feet, and we made our way down the dock and back to the car as fast as we could.

"Darn it," Josie said as we approached my SUV.

"What?"

"They're ruined."

"What on earth are you talking about?"

"The cannoli," she said. "I had the last two in my pocket."

"You're unbelievable," I said, shaking my head.

"Me? Suzy, I should warn you that this isn't a good time for you to start on me."

That was probably good advice.

I started the car and turned the heater on full blast. We shook and shivered as we made the short drive home in silence.

It was too bad about the cannoli.

Then I realized it didn't matter. There was no way Josie was in the mood to share at the moment.

Chapter 9

Like I try to do every day, I said good morning to all our guests, spending a couple of minutes with each dog inside their condo. I should probably point out a few things about life around the Inn. We refer to our dogs as guests because that's what they are. And the word guest reminds everyone, especially our staff, how Josie and I expect them to be treated. The use of the term *condo* is probably a misnomer since our guests stay in enclosures that are only about the size of a small bedroom you might find in a family home. But our guests think they're spacious and plush. At least that's what Josie and I think they think.

We're getting pretty good, but we're still struggling to become fluent in dog.

And just so we're clear, the word cage is forbidden around the Inn.

I think the language we use is important to help set the tone for the type of business we want to operate and to help people understand and appreciate our philosophy and approach. I know Josie agrees with me completely about the importance of language, but you wouldn't be able to tell that this morning.

She still isn't speaking to me.

She'd left the house early this morning without eating breakfast. Since we had Chef Claire's amazing corned beef hash, I knew Josie was still running hot, and I decided to leave her alone this morning. But around nine, I did leave two cream-filled chocolate doughnuts on her desk while she was handling a minor emergency with a black lab who had felt the need to ignore its owner's warning and had gone ahead and tried to play tag with a porcupine that had wandered onto their property.

I touched base with Jill and Sammy, two of our staff who helped us keep the place running smoothly. Since summer was over, the number of boarding guests was down, but our rescue numbers were up substantially. The publicity we'd received from John's generous gift was extensive, and it seemed everyone within a fifty-mile radius was bringing in strays on a daily basis. That was fine with us, and we were already working with a local architect on an expansion to the Inn to accommodate the increased number of rescues.

I watched as Jill leaned over Sammy's shoulder to review a bill with a customer. They were both laughing, and Jill placed a hand on top of Sammy's and left it there. Recently Josie and I had noticed that they were spending a lot of time together and we'd begun to wonder if they had a little thing going on between them. But for now, all my snooping energies were devoted to figuring out who had killed Roger the Engineer and almost done the same to Jackson.

Thinking about Jackson reminded me that I needed to call his father and get an update on his condition. I headed for my office, sat down behind the desk, and made the call. Jackson's dad answered on the second ring.

"Hi, Mr. Frank."

"Suzy, I was just getting ready to call you," he said.

He sounded relatively upbeat, but my stomach still sunk while I waited to hear what he had to say.

"The swelling has gone down, and Jackson's condition has gone from critical to serious. And he's out of intensive care."

"That's great news," I choked out. My eyes filled with tears, and I wiped at them with the back of my hand.

Funny how sometimes it's the good news that turns on the waterworks.

Josie entered the office, and I noticed chocolate frosting on the corner of her mouth. She saw me crying and assumed the worst.

51

"What is it?" she said, sitting down in a chair in front of the desk. "Is it Jackson?"

I nodded and tried to smile, but it wasn't my best effort. I put the phone on speaker and set it down on the desk.

"Josie just came in, Mr. Frank," I said, trying to catch my breath.

"Hi, Josie."

"Good morning, Mr. Frank. Is everything okay?" Josie said, staring down at the phone.

"Yes, I was just telling Suzy that Jackson's condition has improved. They moved him out of intensive care, and he's conscious. I was able to talk with him this morning."

"That's fantastic," Josie said. "When will we be able to see him?"

"Well, the doctor said that he could start having limited visitations. But the visits will have to be very short. Given that, I'm not sure it's worth you making the trip."

I glanced at Josie, and she nodded her head vigorously.

"We'll be there this afternoon," I said.

Mr. Frank laughed softly.

"You two are something else," he said. "I'll tell him you're on your way. I know that will perk him up even more. Oh, he did ask me how Sluggo is doing."

"Tell him Sluggo's fine," Josie said. "And tell Jackson that he's started to lose that five pounds we've been pushing for."

Sluggo's weight loss was understandable since he still hadn't eaten since the incident on the boat.

"I'll do that," he said. "And I guess I'll see you two this afternoon. Bye."

I blew my nose and leaned back in my chair.

"That's great news," I said.

"Yes, it certainly is," Josie said, checking her schedule on her phone. "I can probably be ready to head out by one."

"Good," I said. "That will get us there by two-thirty at the latest."

"That's fine," Josie said, giving me an odd look.

"What?" I finally said.

"Did you really think that I'd forgive you for almost getting us killed last night just by giving me a doughnut?" Josie said.

"No, that's why I brought you two," I said, giving her my best deadpan expression.

She stared at me, then burst into laughter.

"That's better," I said. "Now wipe the chocolate off your mouth."

She headed off to her next appointment, and I busied myself with some paperwork I'd been avoiding for the past couple of days. I called Chef Claire at the house and asked if she would pack a lunch for the car ride. Neither one of us would have time to break for lunch, and a ninety-minute car ride when we were both hungry was neither pleasant nor recommended.

Chef Claire came into the Inn around noon carrying a picnic basket, and for the next hour, it sat on my desk untouched. I congratulated myself on my self-control and waited for Josie to finish up an annual checkup on a Jack Russell terrier that had enough energy to power a small town.

We were on the road by one, and before I got out of the driveway, Josie was digging through the picnic basket.

"What have we got?" I said, feeling my stomach rumble.

"She's so good," Josie said, holding up two long objects wrapped in aluminum foil. "These wraps are perfect for the drive. Chef Claire knows how much you worry about food getting spilled in the car."

It wasn't the food I worried about. It was the Tasmanian Devil eating machine in the passenger seat that concerned me. But since Josie's mood was greatly improved, I decided not to correct her.

Josie worked the aluminum foil loose on one of the wraps and handed it to me. I took a bite and savored it, then realized I'd slowed down from sixty-five to forty. I accelerated back to sixty-five and set the cruise control.

One less thing to worry about.

"Is that dill I'm tasting?" I said.

"Yeah, I think she put it in the mustard-mayo sauce."

"It's incredible. When did she find time to grill the chicken?"

Josie shrugged and grunted as she took another bite.

The traffic remained light, and we finished our sandwiches, munched on cheese wedges and slices of fruit, and polished things off with chocolate chip cookies the size of a small Frisbee. I showed remarkable restraint and stopped at two. Josie said she'd kill me if I told anyone how many she had so I guess you'll just have to use your imagination.

We parked, entered Upstate Medical, and found Jackson's parents sitting outside his room. After everyone had shared hugs, a nurse escorted us into Jackson's room where he was sitting up and watching TV. His head was wrapped in bandages, and he seemed a bit groggy, but his eyes were clear, and he beamed at us as soon as we stepped inside.

I considered that to be a very good sign.

"Hi, Jackson," I said, leaning over to give him a gentle embrace and a kiss on the cheek.

Josie followed suit and then we sat down near his bed. He turned off the television and yawned.

"Thanks for coming, guys," he said. "It's good to see you."

"We've been worried about you," I said.

"I appreciate that. But the doctors say I'm going to be as good as new. I was lucky."

"How long are you going to have to be in the hospital?" Josie said.

"If everything continues to go well, I should be out in less than a week," he said, his eyes drooping. He stifled another yawn. "Sorry. They just gave me a shot, and it always knocks me out."

"Don't worry about it," Josie said. "Just get your rest."

"Have the police been in to talk with you yet?" I said.

"No, but I think they're planning to do that tomorrow. I think everyone has been waiting until I could string a sentence together."

"Did you get a look at who did this to you?" I said.

"No," he said blinking, then giving up the fight and closing his eyes. "After we heard the woman's scream, I raced to the boat and went down below deck to see if anything was going on down there. Then out of nowhere, *bam*, right on the back of the head and I was out."

"What did you see before you got hit?" I said.

"Nothing," he said, managing to get his eyes open. "Not a thing."

"Except for the dead body on the bed," Josie said.

"What dead body?" he said, drifting off to sleep.

I stared at Josie.

"That's odd," she said.

"There's no way he could have missed seeing the body," I said.

"No, you're right," she said.

"This changes things," I said, my mind racing.

Josie shook her head.

"What's the matter?" I said.

"Just the usual stuff," she said.

"What usual stuff?"

"You. And your compulsive behavior when it comes to solving a mystery."

"Well, you have to admit that something in the timeline has changed, right? Maybe that bit of news changes everything."

"Maybe," she said.

"How is it possible for there not to be a body on the bed when Jackson got attacked, and then for it to be there two minutes later when everyone else showed up?"

"I have no idea, Suzy."

"It's like some kind of magic trick," I said. "You know what we need to do, right?"

"Yes," Josie said, shaking her head. "You want to go over everything from the beginning. You want to figure out a way for us to talk with everyone who could have been involved without seeming suspicious. And you want me to call Freddie."

"And?" I said.

"There's more?" she said.

"Yes. And you know what it is."

"No," Josie said, shaking her head.

"Yes, Josie."

Josie shook her head like a two-year-old refusing to eat dinner.

"No way, Suzy," she said.

"Yes. We need to take another shot at having a look around that boat." I said.

"You're unbelievable," Josie whispered.

"Relax," I said. "This time we'll have a more organized plan of attack."

"Oh, that makes me feel so much better," Josie said.

"But this time make sure you put all the snacks you bring along in plastic bags. You know, just in case we end up back in the water," I said, again using my best deadpan expression.

This time, she didn't laugh.

Chapter 10

Freddie X was our county's medical examiner, and we considered him a good friend. He lived in Clay Bay, but since he served the entire county, he spent a lot of time on the local roads determining how various residents had met their demise. Usually, these deaths were caused by accidents or infirmities, but at times he was called in to help investigate a murder.

Like the case of Roger the Engineer.

The guy with the broken neck on the boat that wasn't there when Jackson had arrived on the scene but was on the bed a mere two minutes later after Jackson had been attacked and knocked unconscious.

As you might imagine, ever since Jackson had groggily shared that bit of news with us, I became a bit obsessed, which eventually made Josie extremely cranky and forced her to seek sanctuary in the condos. I found her hiding behind Tiny, a Great Dane that had been dropped off at the Inn in the middle of the night a couple of years ago. Now he was one of the fifteen dogs we considered ours and off the list of dogs eligible for adoption. As far as Josie and I were concerned, Tiny was already rescued.

Josie made the call and later that afternoon we headed for Freddie's office that was next door to the hospital and not far from the police station. That's one of the things I like about living here. Nothing is very far from anywhere.

We parked right in front, and when I climbed out of the SUV, I felt a brisk north wind hit me in the face. My eyes watered, and I flipped my collar up and scrunched over as I trotted toward the door. Judging from the way Josie laughed, my trot must have looked more like a wind-aided stagger.

I so need to get to the gym.

But you can work up quite a sweat trying to walk through a thirty mile an hour north wind with gusts to forty. Technically, it wasn't a workout, but I'm going to count it.

I should point out that I love pretty much everything that comes out of Canada including the people, the music, their beer, and hockey. But on many days, I wished they could figure out a way to keep the north wind to themselves.

Ever since Josie arrived in town four years ago to open the Inn with me, Freddie had his eyes on being more than friends with her. But Josie continued to politely refuse any and all of his requests for dates that might lead to bigger things. One day I asked Freddie why he always asked her to go to lunch or dinner, instead of trying another approach with something simpler like taking a nice walk or maybe going for a boat ride. He responded by saying that his chances with Josie were minuscule, and if he removed the prospect of a good meal from the equation, he knew whatever chance he did have would completely evaporate.

I like the way he thinks.

And I had to admire his tenacity.

The guy is tireless on the Josie front.

Right now, I was witnessing another of Freddie's attempts at weaseling a date out of her. As always, Josie gently and politely deflected it away. But Freddie had stopped by Paterson's bakery and picked up a box of their brownies.

Score a point for our local M.E.

I finished my second brownie and turned all business.

"Josie said she mentioned over the phone what Jackson told us," I said.

"You mean about how the body wasn't on the bed when he got there?" Freddie said, leaning back in his chair.

"Yeah," I said. "Do you think that's possible?"

"Gee, I don't know, Suzy," he said, shaking his head. "I'm not sure there was enough time. Whoever did it must have heard people running along the dock, right? They would have had only had a minute or two tops before someone else showed up. Maybe Jackson's mistaken. He's been through a lot."

"Maybe," I said, nodding. "The cause of death was the broken neck, right?"

"Yeah, pretty much," he said.

"Pretty much?" I said, raising an eyebrow at him. "Is that the technical term?"

"Relax, Suzy," he said. "I was just trying to lighten the mood. Look, in cases like these, when the spinal cord is severely injured, and the injury occurs at or above C5, breathing can be affected. The portion of the spinal cord that controls breathing runs through that area of the spinal cord.

"C5 is the name of a vertebra isn't it?" I said.

"Yes, the fifth cervical vertebra," Freddie said. "When the injury is in that spot the person can die from asphyxiation. That's what happened to Roger."

"You're sure?" I said.

"I'll go 99.9% sure," Freddie said, shaking his head. "How's that?"

"So there is a chance it was something else," I said.

Josie snorted and stared out the window.

"I'm just trying to make sure we don't miss anything," I said, glancing back and forth at them.

"I think you're safe to proceed with whatever you're doing under the assumption that Roger died from a broken neck," Freddie said. "By the way, what are you doing?"

"Nothing," I said.

Josie sighed audibly and looked at Freddie.

"Was there an autopsy done on the body?" she said.

"No, it was pretty clear what happened, and his family didn't want one," Freddie said.

Josie nodded as she stood and reached for another brownie.

"Thanks, Freddie," Josie said, zipping up her coat. "Ready to go, Miss Marples?"

"Funny," I said, pulling on my jacket. "Thanks, Freddie. By the way, we're going to be having a little welcome home party for Jackson at the house when he gets back."

"I'm in. Just let me know," Freddie said. "Should I bring anything?"

I looked at Josie who was polishing off the last of her brownie. I glanced at Freddie and pointed at the empty box.

"Another box of those probably couldn't hurt," I said.

Outside, the wind was howling even harder, and we slowly made our way back to the car, and I turned on the heater.

"I know it's still only September, but I think that it might be a good night for a fire. Chloe is going to love sleeping in front of the fireplace," I said.

"Hmmm," Josie said, staring out the window.

"I hate to start using it this early, but what can you do, right?"

"Yeah," she said, rubbing her forehead.

I glanced over at her. I had no idea where she was at the moment. It certainly wasn't here in the car.

"And I'm thinking about rubbing suntan lotion over my naked body in front of the fire to see if I can get an early start on my winter tan," I said.

"That's nice," she said, then snapped to attention. "What did you say?"

"Earth to Josie," I said, laughing.

"Sorry," she said. "I was just thinking about something."

"Really? I hadn't noticed," I said, turning into our driveway. "What's on your mind?"

"I was just sitting here thinking that it would be impossible to get Roger the Engineer's body on the bed after Jackson was attacked."

"Go on," I said, nodding.

"There was so much blood on the floor," she said.

"Yes, there was."

"And while the floor space below deck is big for a boat, it certainly couldn't be called spacious."

"No, it couldn't," I said.

"And if someone had killed Roger or even tried to position the body on the bed, there should have been bloody footprints all over the place."

"Yes, there would have to be," I said, coming to a stop in front of the house and turning the car off.

"Suzy?"

"Yeah."

"You already figured all that out, didn't you?"

"Yup."

"Why didn't you mention it?"

"Would you have believed me if I had?" I said, climbing out of the car.

"No," Josie said.

"Well, there you go."

I smiled as I climbed the steps. When it came to Josie, sometimes you just had to be patient and wait for her to figure things out. Eventually, she always got there.

I'm not sure that strategy was going to work for Freddie, but it was probably the only chance he had.

Chapter 11

Chef Claire called it her version of a potluck supper. All of the dishes were common at communal gatherings, but the difference was that Chef Claire had done all the cooking. We'd come up with the idea after running into Captain Bill, Alice, and the two other members of the crew we hadn't met yet at the grocery store. They'd been bemoaning the fact that all of them were stuck in a motel until the boat was ready for its trip to Florida and that their ability to do any real cooking was limited.

I thought having all of them over for dinner was the neighborly thing to do. Josie thought I was simply trying to get them in the same place for several hours to see if any of them slipped up and divulged incriminating information.

Tomato, tomahto.

I surveyed the kitchen with Chloe at my heels. The smells were sending her into a frenzy. I wasn't far behind. Josie was pacing the kitchen like an expectant father and kept casting loving stares at the stove.

Chef Claire was taking advantage of the cold weather to put together a comfort meal menu. On the stove were three large pots. In one of the pots was a ham and spinach cream soup I'd tasted earlier. It was a total knee-buckler. In another pot, there was a turkey and pork belly chili I hadn't been able to get my hands on yet. But it smelled fantastic. In the third pot was a beef stew that had my name all over it and I was tempted to go in for a sample despite the fact that Chef Claire was holding a large knife and giving me a hard stare.

"Don't you guys have work to do?" Chef Claire said.

"Not really," I said.

"No, I'm good," Josie said.

Chloe barked once and sat down staring up at Chef Claire.

"She gets that from her mother," Josie said, laughing.

"Let's try this. Why don't you guys grab the tray that's on the top shelf of the fridge and head for the living room?" Chef Claire said, turning back to the stove.

Josie removed the tray and set it down on the table. She removed the foil and stared at it.

"Is that what I think it is?" I said.

"Yes," Chef Claire said. "That's my famous cold appetizer tray you've heard so much about."

I stared down at the collection. Roasted red peppers bathing in olive oil and garlic. Deviled eggs with bacon and scallions. Hummus and a host of other dips and salsas. A variety of sliced vegetables along with other assorted items I wouldn't be able to identify until I tasted them. Chef Claire removed a loaf of fresh bread from the oven and sliced it. She arranged the bread around the edge of the tray then pointed at the living room.

"Now go," she said, laughing. "What a couple of mooches you two are."

I followed Josie out of the kitchen, and we sat down on a couch with the tray in front of us on the coffee table. I gently shooed Chloe toward the fireplace, and she stretched out and was soon asleep in front of the fire. Sluggo was already there and barely looked up. He still hadn't eaten, and I was getting a bit concerned, but Josie kept reminding me that a healthy dog wouldn't starve itself to death.

I carefully draped one of the roasted red peppers on a piece of warm bread and tossed it back. Josie had decided on full frontal assault on the deviled eggs. Five minutes later, we took a short break and a sip of wine. We sat back and sighed.

"Unbelievable," I said.

"So good," Josie said. "You know, it's probably not a good idea for Chef Claire to reward our hovering like this."

"Yeah," I said, leaning forward to grab one of the eggs. "If this is our punishment, I'm going to buy a hoverboard."

A car pulled into the driveway, and I got up and headed for the front door. I looked out through the window and saw Captain Bill towering over his three companions. I'd forgotten what a large man he was. I opened the door, and the four members of the crew stepped inside and removed their jackets. We exchanged greetings, and I handled coat duty while Josie poured the wine. Alice got reacquainted with Chloe, but only got a mild snort out of Sluggo.

"So, do you folks have a departure date yet?" I said, settling back on the couch.

"No," Captain Bill said, helping himself to the appetizers. "But the police did finish up today, so it's no longer a crime scene."

"Well, that's good news. Now you can start the renovations, right?" I said.

Captain Bill stared at me, then glanced around at the other members of his crew. I recognized their confusion and felt the need to explain myself.

"John told us that the owner in Florida changed his mind and wanted to do something different below deck."

"Yes, he does," Captain Bill said, reaching for a deviled egg.

"Such a pity," Josie said. "I thought the marble and wood looked fantastic."

"Yeah," Alice said, helping herself to a small plate of hummus and sliced veggies. "It's just too heavy." She paused and looked around. "Sometimes heavy is good, other times not so much."

Captain Bill chewed slowly and looked at Alice. She caught his eye and blushed. Then she flashed him a smile. He gave her a nervous cough in return. I glanced at Josie. She'd caught the exchange as well. I think we may have just figured out the identity of the amorous couple on the boat with the shotgun.

Good for them I decided. It was a long way to Florida and, after all, how much reading could one do?

I turned to the other two members of the crew. They were in their early twenties, both very good looking and obviously a couple. They shared a plate of food like two people married for twenty years. The young man, who went by the name of Axel, looked around the living room.

"This is a great house," he said. "And the big building down the hill is where you keep all the dogs?"

"Yes," Josie said. "That's an interesting accent. Where are you from?"

"I'm originally from Portugal, but moved to Montreal when I was a kid."

"I love Montreal," I said.

"Yeah, I like it," he said. "I hadn't planned on staying there, but when I met Sheila a couple of years ago, my plans changed in a hurry."

Sheila blushed and squeezed Axel's hand. He beamed at her and stroked the side of her face with the back of his hand.

Maybe I needed to reconsider the identity of the couple on the boat.

"So do you guys work on boats full-time?" Josie said.

"We have been," Axel said. "But after we finish this trip, Sheila and I are going to take an extended break and try to figure out what we want to do next."

"I'd go crazy if I were stuck on a boat all the time," Josie said.

"Yeah, it can get old after a while," Sheila said.

It was the first time she'd spoken, and I detected a hint of a French accent.

Since she was from Montreal, I really couldn't take much credit for figuring that one out.

"Not for me," Captain Bill said. "Being on the water is the only time I feel alive. And being stuck here is driving me crazy." He glanced back and forth at Josie and me. "I didn't mean that like it sounded. It's a nice town, but I need to get back on the water."

"No offense taken," I said, laughing. "So where are you from originally, Captain Bill?"

He shrugged. "I was born in Florida. But I was in the Navy for a long time and was all over the place. Europe, the Mideast, Asia. You name the place, chances are I've been there. Especially if it's warm. It's getting downright cold around here at night. Especially on that boat."

I changed my mind and went back to my first guess. Captain Bill and Alice were definitely the couple on the boat.

"Tell me about it," Axel said. "And it's still only September."

I glanced back and forth between the two men. If I didn't know better, I'd swear they were trying to mess with my detective intuitions.

"I don't like being on that boat at night," Alice said, breaking the silence. "After what happened there, it gives me the creeps."

"You'll get used to it," Captain Bill said.

"Who knows who might be lurking around?" Alice said.

"Nobody is lurking anywhere," Captain Bill said, shaking his head. "Maybe a couple of nosy kids or some local yokels trying to sneak a peek at the boat, but that's it."

I've been called nosy many times, and now it rolled off me like water off a duck's back. And it had been a long time since I'd been called a kid.

But local yokel was a first. I didn't like the term. I glanced at Josie and could tell she wasn't fond of the expression either.

"Maybe you're right," Alice said. "But I still don't like being there after dark."

"Just hang in there," Captain Bill said. "We'll be on the water before you know it.

I nodded my head. The answer to the final Jeopardy question of *The name of the couple on the boat with a shotgun* is: Who are Captain Bill and Alice?"

I glanced at Axel and Sheila and got even further confirmation that I was correct. The way they continued to hold hands and stare into each other's eyes convinced me that, at night, they probably had a hard time ever getting out of the motel.

And if we happened to leave them alone for too long tonight, they might have a hard time making it out of the living room.

Chapter 12

"Suzy, I'm not saying no," Josie said, sliding open the door to Tiny's condo and stepping inside to give the massive Great Dane a bear hug. "How's my big boy today?"

Seconds later, Josie was on her back laughing as she fought off Tiny's answer to her question. He pinned her shoulders to the floor with his front paws and nestled his head against her neck. A long trail of slobber hung from her ear when she finally managed to climb to her feet. She wiped the drool away and played a quick game of tuggy using the towel as the toy. The game didn't last long because Tiny snatched the towel out of her hand and stood waiting for her to try to grab it.

We were making our usual morning rounds and stopping by each condo to say good morning to our guests and conduct a quick check to make sure they were all alert and in good spirits. Our progress was slow today since we were still discussing last night's dinner with the boat crew and debating our next steps. I rubbed Tiny's head and let him put his paws up on my shoulders and waited until he had finished licking my hands and face.

"Yes," I said, laughing as I finally managed to squirm away. "It's nice to see you, Tiny."

We closed the door and headed to the adjacent condo where a two-year-old Beagle named Louie with a bad foot sat waiting thumping his tail on the tile floor. Josie knelt down to examine the bandage.

"So, if you're not saying no, that means yes, right?" I said.

I thought my logic was irrefutable. Not bad for seven-thirty in the morning.

Josie rose to her feet and made a note on the Beagle's chart that hung outside the door.

"No means not now," Josie said. "I'm not going back on that boat at night until I'm positive there's no one around."

"There's risk in everything," I said.

"My point exactly. I think it's important to minimize the degree of risk one takes whenever possible. And that's a little hard to do when getting blasted by a shotgun is part of the equation."

Josie glanced over her shoulder as Jill and Sammy entered pushing carts that held large bags of dog food and various treats. They were giggling about something, and they returned Josie's wave as they approached.

"Morning, guys," I said.

"Hey, Suzy. Morning, Josie," Jill said.

They came to a stop in front of us, flashed a quick smile at each other, then waited for Josie to give them her notes on what's she'd discovered on her morning rounds.

"Sammy, we need to put a fresh bandage on Louie. I was hoping he'd leave it alone, but he's chewed right through it."

"I'm sorry about that, Josie," Sammy said, glancing at the Beagle.

"No, it's not your fault," she said. "I forgot to put it in my notes. It's my mistake. After you get the fresh one on, spray it with a healthy dose of the yuk juice. And this time, I suggest that you believe me when I tell you not to sample it."

Jill and I stifled a laugh. The yuk juice was a safe, yet incredibly bitter, concoction that Josie had created to keep dogs from chewing or licking bandages and hot spots. A few months ago despite Josie's warning, Sammy had convinced himself that it couldn't taste that bad and had sprayed some on his tongue. Two days later he was still complaining and worried that his sense of taste would never return.

"It should work, but if it doesn't we'll need to consider putting a cone on Louie," Josie said, checking her notes. "And make sure the cocker spaniel in seventeen eats this morning, okay? She's been off her food since the surgery. Everyone else seems good so just follow the schedule we discussed at our wrap up yesterday."

"Got it," Sammy said, turning to Jill. "Which side do you want to start from?"

"I'll take that end," Jill said, pointing at the far wall.

"Cool. I'll meet you in the middle," Sammy said, rolling his breakfast cart in the opposite direction.

We watched as they grinned at each other, then headed for my office.

"I think their romance is official," Josie said, stretching out on the couch.

"Yeah. Good for them," I said, rummaging through my desk until I found what I was looking for. I held both of the objects up. "I've got Fig Newtons and Oreos. Which one do you want?"

"The Fig Newtons are probably the healthier breakfast choice, right?"

"Probably," I said, laughing.

She pondered the decision for about two seconds.

"Ah, the heck with it," she said. "I'll take the Oreos."

I tossed her the pack of cookies and started opening my own.

"So what's your take on last night?" I said, popping a Fig Newton into my mouth.

"It was incredible," she said, dunking an Oreo into her coffee.

"That's disgusting," I said, watching as she chewed the coffee-drenched cookie.

"I think the beef stew was my favorite," she said, reaching for another Oreo and repeating the dunk move.

"Yes, we all noticed," I said. "I wasn't referring to the food."

"I know what you were referring to," she said, wiping her mouth. "It's just that it's a little early in the morning to try solving a murder."

If Josie was trying to send me a not so subtle hint that she didn't want to talk about a list of potential suspects, it didn't work. I decided I needed to talk through some of the thoughts that had been rolling around my head since last night and continued.

"I'm just not sure about Captain Bill. He plays the old salty seadog role to perfection, but I think there's something going on with him."

"There is," Josie said. "And it's Alice."

"Oh, good. You caught that," I said. "What tipped you off?"

"At first it was the way they looked at each other. Then when she made a comment about how sometimes heavy is good, and other times it isn't, I caught her winking at him."

"Yeah, I noticed," I said. "Well, Captain Bill is a big guy. Maybe she's into heavy."

"But he's very solid," Josie said. "And obviously strong as an ox."

"He's certainly strong enough to snap someone's neck," I said.

"Yup."

"He's cute in a weird way," I said.

"Yeah, I guess. He's not my type, but I can see why Alice might go for him," Josie said. "She told me one time during the summer that she's into older guys." She paused to look at me before continuing. "And I think she and Jackson might have had a little thing going on for a while."

"No way," I said, stunned by the comment. "Jackson and Alice? Really?"

"Yeah, you saw last night how devastated she still is about what happened to him. Every time Jackson's name came up, tears started rolling down her cheeks. And think about it. All those long hours when they were working together. Plus all the time they spent together alone on the police boat. There are lots of places on the River you can go if you want to spend some time alone without anyone knowing about it, right?"

"Yes, there certainly are," I said, knowing where many of them were from growing up in the area. "Did Alice ever say anything about Jackson to you?"

"No, of course not," Josie said. "But the way they interacted changed as the summer went along. They were very chummy for a while and then it seemed to cool off. I just assumed it ended when Jackson realized that it wasn't a good idea to be involved with his intern."

"Jackson wouldn't do that," I said, shaking my head.

"Maybe not," Josie said. "But she's a very attractive young woman. And while Jackson is a lot older than she is, it's not outside the boundaries. I've seen much bigger age differences."

"That's because you've been hanging around my mother," I said, making a mental note to give her a call.

Josie laughed.

"How old do you think Captain Bill is?" I said.

Josie thought about it, then shrugged.

"I'd guess forty something. Maybe a bit younger," Josie said. "It's hard to tell. The sun and wind have taken a toll on him."

"That's probably what gives him that rugged look," I said.

"He's on the suspect list, right?"

"Oh, yeah," I said. "He's definitely on it. What's your take on Axel and Sheila?"

"Young love that's still basking in the initial glow of lust," Josie said.

"But they said they'd been together for two years," I said. "Shouldn't some of that have worn off by now?"

"Maybe it has," Josie said.

"Now that's a scary thought," I said, laughing.

"Maybe they both just got lucky and found the perfect partner," Josie said, laughing along. "It happens. Or so I hear."

"I can't see either one of them as a killer," I said.

"Me neither," Josie said. "For them, I think this boat trip to Florida is just an adventure with a paycheck."

"Good description," I said. "An adventure with a paycheck. It must be nice to be young and carefree."

"I guess. I always thought it was a bit overrated, but they seem happy."

"So the couple is off the list?" I said.

"Well, let's not take them completely off it yet. Maybe the paycheck is a lot bigger than we realize at the moment. But I'd be shocked if either one of them was involved," Josie said.

"Yeah, so would I," I said. "Okay, first things first. Let's see if we can figure out a way to get back on that boat."

"You mean, figure out a *safe* way to get back on it, right?"

"Of course. That goes without saying. I don't want to get shot any more than you do," I said, getting up to refill our coffees.

"I'm so glad to hear that," she said, laughing.

"But how can we make sure we're safe?" I said.

Josie sat up on the couch and tucked her legs underneath her. She took a sip of coffee and stared at the collection of dog photos we had hung on one of the walls.

"I guess one way to be sure would be to start with a list of all the people who have any reason to be on the boat," she said.

"Go on," I said, nodding.

"And then the next thing would be to make sure we knew exactly where they all were before we tried sneaking back on."

"I think I like where this is going," I said, leaning forward and putting my elbows on the desk.

"You do?" Josie said. "I'm just babbling. I don't have a clue what I'm talking about."

"No, you're on the right track," I said. "If we can figure out a way to get everyone in the same place at the same time, we'd be able to get on the boat and take our time."

"And not have to worry about getting shot," Josie said.

"Yeah, that would be nice," I said. "But how do we pull that off?"

Josie thought for a moment and then slowly nodded her head.

"It's like they taught us in scouting. When you're facing a challenge, do your best to understand the tools at your disposal, and then use them to your full advantage," Josie said.

"You were in the Girl Scouts?"

"Actually, I never made it past the Brownies," she said, frowning. "That group turned out to be something completely different from their name."

I roared with laughter.

"No way," I said.

"Yeah," she said, laughing. "I thought it was a food club. Boy, was I wrong. But the snacks were pretty good."

"Okay, Josie the Brownie, what tools do we have at our disposal?"

"The way I see it, we have three. We have the ability to create interest in an event, we have the ability to maintain interest in that event, and we have the opportunity to create subterfuge."

"English please," I said, taking a sip of coffee.

"Jackson will be coming home soon, right?"

"Yes. By the end of the week at the latest," I said, nodding.

"We've already talked about throwing him a welcome home party."

"And we'll be inviting everyone, right?"

"Correct. And everyone will love the chance to see Jackson," Josie said. "Step one complete. Create interest."

"But the boat crew, apart from Alice, doesn't know him," I said.

"No, but that takes us right into Step two. You saw how much they loved Chef Claire's food last night."

"Well, it was a bit hard at times to see through the sparks your knife and fork were throwing off, but yeah."

"Funny. And this from the woman who polished off three bowls of chili and half a baking sheet of jalapeno cornbread," Josie said, glaring at me. "All we need to do is get the word out that Chef Claire will be catering the party and they'll be there. And if we work with Chef Claire to stagger her menu that will solve all our Step Two problems."

"Maintaining interest?"

"Correct," Josie said.

"What do you mean by stagger?"

"On the invitation, we can say something like Chef Claire will be serving her famous whatever at eight o'clock, then her next famous whatever at nine, and so on."

"That's perfect. Nobody would leave the party early for fear of missing out."

"It's highly unlikely," Josie said. "That leaves us with Step Three, creating subterfuge."

"That's an easy one," I said. "All we'd need to do would be to create a fake dog emergency and leave the party to deal with it."

"Well done. You got it in one. We can just leave a car down at the Inn and drive into town from there. Nobody would be the least bit suspicious."

"No, they wouldn't," I said. "In fact, our leaving a party to take care of a sick dog is exactly what everyone would expect us to do."

"Plus, they'll all be thinking, more food for me," Josie said, laughing.

"How long do you think we'll need to explore the boat?" I said, frowning.

"I have no idea," Josie said. "Why do you ask?"

"I'd just hate to miss out on any of Chef Claire's famous whatevers."

Chapter 13

"Good morning, Jackson," I said, beaming at him.

"You're looking good," Josie said, following me to his bedside.

"Hi, guys," Jackson said, sitting up even further. "Thanks, Josie. How good would that be?"

Jackson gave her a coy smile, folded his arms across his chest, and struck a pose.

"Not that good," Josie said, laughing. "You must be feeling better."

"Much better. And thanks for coming," he said.

His head was still bandaged but all the tubes and monitors he'd been hooked up to the last time we were here were gone. His eyes were clear and focused on the box I was holding.

"Is that a Paterson's box?" he said.

"It is," I said. "We have a dozen of their famous chocolate chip cookies for you."

"You shouldn't have," he said, accepting the box.

"We didn't," I said. "Actually, we bought two dozen." I glanced at Josie, who was doing her best to ignore me. "Somebody couldn't control herself on the drive down."

"Hey," Josie said, "You ate three. And I was the one who suggested we get two dozen just in case, remember?"

Jackson laughed then winced and touched the bandage on his head.

"Dang headaches," he whispered. "The doctor said I should expect to have them for a while."

"Can we get you anything?" I said.

"No, I'm due for my meds in a few minutes," he said, shifting around to get more comfortable. "Man, this place is getting old. I can't wait to get out of here on Friday."

"You think you might be up for a little homecoming party on Saturday night at our place?" Josie said.

"Absolutely," he said. "Who's coming?"

"Everybody," I said. "At least everyone's been invited."

"Should I bring anything?"

"Just your appetite," I said. "Chef Claire is doing the catering."

"That sounds great," he said.

"We invited the crew from the boat," I said.

"They're still around? I thought they'd be long gone by now," he said.

"Well, the police had it designated as a crime scene for a while. Now John's doing some renovations," I said.

"Renovations? The boat's brand new," he said, frowning.

"Apparently the owner in Florida wanted some changes," Josie said.

"Rich people, huh?" he said with a chuckle.

"Alice will be at the party," I said.

"Alice? That's great. It'll be good to see her," Jackson said.

I watched him carefully for any sign of emotional turmoil about the prospect of seeing someone Josie suspected was an ex-girlfriend. But I couldn't detect anything.

Either it didn't bother him, he was hiding how he really felt, or they had never dated.

Geez, that narrows it down. Nice job, Suzy. Having totally whiffed on that one, I decided to move to a new topic.

"How well did you know Roger the Engineer?" I said.

"Not very well at all. I'd met him a few times," Jackson said. "But I think he spent most of his time at John's manufacturing operation in Montreal. Apparently, he's considered a world class boat designer."

"Was," Josie said.

"Yeah," Jackson said, nodding. "You got a point there."

"Do you have any idea who'd want to kill him?" I said.

"Not a clue," he said, shaking his head. Then he paused and stared at both of us. "Hang on a minute. You guys have been snooping, haven't you?"

"No," I said.

"Absolutely not," Josie said, glancing down at the floor.

Jackson maintained his stare and waited. Eventually, I caved like a bad soufflé.

"Well, maybe a little," I whispered.

"Here we go again. You guys are unbelievable," he said. "Okay. Then you might as well give me the update."

"We don't have much at the moment," I said.

"Just a long and ever growing list of potential suspects, right?" he said.

"No," I said, protesting. "It's not that long."

Josie and Jackson both burst out laughing. Mildly offended, I waited until they finished.

"We think it has something to do with the boat," I said.

"Suzy thinks it has something to do with the boat," Josie said. "I'm just going along with her at the moment to keep her out of trouble."

"Good luck with that," Jackson said, laughing.

I'm glad that Jackson is feeling better and all that, but he was starting to make me a bit cranky.

"Thanks for the support," I said, staring at Josie.

"Anytime," she said, punching me gently on the arm.

"I think Captain Bill might have something to do with it," I said.

He considered the idea and then shrugged.

"I wouldn't have a clue what possible motive he could have had to kill Roger," Jackson said. "But he's certainly big enough to have put this dent in my head. What's John's take on this thing?"

"He doesn't seem to have any idea about who might have done it. But he's been busy trying to get things wrapped up for the year, and I'm not sure he's had much time to focus on it," I said.

"That makes sense," Jackson said. "I'm sure he can't wait to get that boat delivered and get paid for it. He must have millions buried in that thing."

A nurse carrying a tray entered and approached the bed.

"Hello, ladies," she said. "I'm afraid you'll need to wrap things up soon. I need to get this guy down for a nap."

Then she spied the box.

"Oh, is that a box from Paterson's in Clay Bay?" she said.

"It is indeed," Jackson said. "Chocolate chip cookies."

"Yum," she said, glancing at us. "My family has a place on the River. Every time I visit Clay Bay, Paterson's is always one of my first stops."

"Have one," Jackson said, extending the box toward her.

"Don't mind if I do," she said, taking a cookie. "Thanks."

Jackson noticed Josie hovering near the box and looked at her.

"Would you like one, Josie?" he said.

"I really shouldn't," she said, reaching for a cookie.

"Suzy?"

I stared at the box, glanced at Josie who was already halfway through hers, then nodded and reached for a cookie.

"Maybe just one for the road," I said.

Chapter 14

When we arrived back in Clay Bay, we headed straight for John's office. His assistant told us he was on the boat checking on the progress of the renovations, so Josie and I made our way down the dock, then up the stairway. We moved to the middle of the deck and glanced around.

"Don't fall in," Josie said.

"Funny," I said.

I headed for the door that led below deck. Unlike our previous visit, the door was wide open. We walked down a small set of stairs and found John talking with a man I assumed to be the supervisor of the other four men who were busy installing new cabinets.

"Look, John," the man said. "I don't know what to tell you. We're doing everything we can, but we still need to find four more."

Sensing our presence, he glanced in our direction and stopped talking. His mouth remained halfway open.

Josie strikes again.

John noticed the expression on the man's face, turned around and smiled at us.

"Hey, guys," John said. "I just got the invitation this morning. I'll be there Saturday night."

"That's great," I said, then glanced at the other man. "Are you going to be, okay?"

His face flushed red, and he stammered something unintelligible. He looked at John who laughed then did introductions. The man did, in fact, turn out to be the supervisor of the work crew.

It was nice to see that my detective skills were as sharp as ever.

"It's nice to meet you," the supervisor eventually managed, sneaking another nervous glance at Josie.

"What can I do for you guys?" John said.

"Oh, we just thought we'd swing by and say hi," I said.

"Of course you did," John said, laughing. "And I'm running for Pope." He turned back to the supervisor. "I'm going up on deck to chat with these two beautiful women."

"I can't blame you for that," the supervisor said.

"And when I'm finished I'm coming back, and I'll be expecting an answer. Are we clear?"

The supervisor nodded and walked off to join the rest of his crew. John pointed toward the deck and bounced up the stairs.

We followed.

My ascent was less than bouncy.

At the top of the stairs, I paused to take a couple of deep breaths.

"Really? You must be joking. It's only four steps," Josie said, shaking her head.

"Shut up," I said, stretching on a deck chair next to where John was already sitting.

"So what's up?" John said, pulling a sweater over his head.

"We were just wondering if you've heard anything from the police about the murder or the attack on Jackson," I said.

"No," he said, shaking his head. "They've got a long list of potential suspects, including the three of us I imagine, but apparently they haven't had any luck linking anybody to it. Why do you ask?"

"Oh, we're just being nosy," Josie said, laughing.

"I'm shocked," John said, glancing back and forth at us.

"Actually, we wanted to run something by you that Jackson mentioned," I said.

"How's he doing?"

"He's good," I said. "We just got back from visiting him. He's coming home Friday."

"That's great news," John said. "Jackson's a good guy. So what did he say?"

"Well, it's strange," I said. "We were asking Jackson if he had seen anything before getting hit in the head and he said no."

"Okay," John said, nodding. "And?"

"And when I said nothing except the dead body," Josie said. "Jackson said what dead body."

"What?"

"Yeah," I said. "Weird, huh?"

"Yes, it certainly is. Let's see. We were on the stage doing the check presentation when we heard the scream. And Jackson was the first person on the boat, and a couple of minutes later we found him unconscious on the floor and Roger's body sprawled out on the bed."

"Yes," I said, nodding.

"Is Jackson sure the body wasn't there?"

"Yes, he's positive," Josie said.

"Let me think this through," John said, leaning back in his chair. "It couldn't have been more than two minutes before the rest of us showed up at the boat, right?"

"At the most," I said.

"I guess Roger could have walked in when Jackson got attacked. And then he was killed right after that," John said, glancing back and forth at us with a frown. "Does that make any sense?"

"Maybe," I said.

"I suppose it's possible," Josie said. "But what about the scream? It was a woman's voice."

"You know, I've been wondering about that myself," John said. "Let me float an idea past you to see if it sounds plausible. You know how sound travels over water, right?"

"Sure," I said. "It tends to echo. And sometimes if the wind is just right, it can be hard to figure out exactly what direction it's coming from."

"Yeah," he said. "And I remember correctly, it was loud but didn't the scream sound kind of muffled?"

"Maybe," I said, searching my memory bank.

"Given what we found when we got to the boat, everyone just made the assumption that it was some woman on the boat who screamed," John said, shaking his head. "Is it possible that it came from someplace else and the two things aren't connected at all?"

"I never even considered that," I said, deflated.

Not only did I think it was possible, I think John might have uncovered an important fact.

A major whiff on my part.

"But even if the scream and the murder aren't connected, it still doesn't help us figure out who did it," John said.

"No," I said, my mind racing.

Maybe racing was stretching the truth a bit. But it was certainly moving a lot faster than I'd climbed the stairs.

I so need to get to the gym.

"You think I should mention it to the police?" John said.

"Maybe," Josie said. "I'm not sure it will help solve the case, but it is a bit of a twist to what we've been thinking."

"Yeah," John said, climbing out of his chair. "Look, I need to get back down there. These guys are way behind schedule."

"Good luck finding four more," I said.

"What?" John said, staring at me like I was an alien.

"When we came in, I heard the supervisor say he needed to find four more."

"Oh, that," John said, shaking his head. "Four more workers. I told him I wanted this job wrapped up by early next week at the latest and he said he'd need four more people to get it done that fast."

"That makes sense," I said.

"But apparently, he's having trouble finding four people with the right skills," John said, laughing. "Can you believe it? The things I need to deal with. Okay, I'll see you two Saturday night. I can't wait to see what Chef Claire comes up with."

"Me either," Josie said.

"Don't fall in climbing down the stairs," he said, laughing. "It's really cold at the moment."

"What were you doing in the water?" Josie said.

"I went waterskiing. I thought I could handle one last run. Boy, was I wrong."

He waved goodbye and headed below deck.

We climbed back down the stairway that led to the dock.

And in case you're wondering, trust me, I took my sweet time.

Chapter 15

The possibility that the woman's scream had come from somewhere other than the boat tormented me all day. And since it was tormenting me, that meant I was tormenting Josie with endless questions and what ifs. Fortunately for her, she had a couple of afternoon surgeries and a handful of annual exams to deal with and was finally able to escape my obsessive behavior.

I wasn't so lucky and continued to work myself into a frenzy.

I thought myself in a circle, then into a corner, wore myself out, and still came up empty. I decided the question of what woman had screamed and where she'd had been at the time could wait. So I went back to the main issue of who had killed Roger the Engineer and hit Jackson in the back of the head with a wrench.

Then I wondered if one person had committed both crimes or if two different people were involved. By the time I was done, I had managed to convince myself that there might be a large international conspiracy at work and that the FBI and CIA would have to be called in to assist with the investigation.

Then I got a headache, ate a handful of chocolate, and decided to take Chloe for a walk before it started to rain.

We had just stepped outside when I saw my mother drive into the parking lot outside the Inn. She kicked up her usual amount of dust and gravel, and I waited for it to settle before heading towards her car.

"Hello, darling," she said.

For her, she was dressed casually. Jeans, boots, bulky sweater, and a wool scarf. But the ensemble was color coordinated and, as always, she looked fantastic.

"Hi, Mom. What's up?"

"Can't I just stop by to say hi to my daughter?" she said, frowning.

"Sure you can," I said. "It's just that you never do."

"Be that as it may, I just stopped by to see if it's okay for me to bring somebody to your party," she said, glancing up at the threatening sky.

"Of course," I said. "But you know you don't need to ask."

"No, I know that," she said. "I just thought I should probably check with you first as a courtesy."

I stared at her. She was acting a bit strange about something that didn't even need discussion.

"Hot date?" I said, chuckling.

"It's a bit more than that, darling," she said. "I think I may have found a keeper."

"Really? You?"

"Does that somehow strike you as funny?" she said.

"Yeah, it does. Aren't you the one who always says, *never keep 'em, lose before weepin'?*"

I always laughed when she said it since I thought it was a clever twist to the old Finders Keepers rhyme. And it perfectly summed up her approach to dating.

"I do not say that," she snapped. "And if you mention it Saturday night, I will vigorously deny it."

"Relax, Mom," I said, laughing. "Your secret is safe with me. Who is he?"

"He's a delightful man who owns a large foreign car dealership outside of Rochester," she said.

"That makes sense," I said, nodding at her new Mercedes. "After all, you two must have been spending a lot of time together the past few months."

"Funny, darling," she said. "So what's new? We haven't spoken in a few days."

"Yeah, sorry about that," I said. "We've been pretty focused on what happened to Jackson."

"You mean you've been snooping, right?"

"Maybe," I said, taking a tennis ball out of my pocket.

Chloe went on point, barked once, and sat down staring at the ball in my hand.

"You want to come for a walk with us?"

I threw the ball across the lawn and watched Chloe race after it.

"No, darling. I have to get my car into the dealership."

"Geez, Mom, I said, shaking my head. "You don't need to buy another new car. Why don't you just meet him for a drink like a normal person?"

"No, that's not it. It's making a rattling sound, and I can't for the life of me figure out where it's coming from," she said.

"It's probably just that bottle I hid in your trunk."

"Funny, darling."

She stared at me until she was convinced I was joking.

I reached down to grab the ball Chloe had dropped at my feet. I fired it across the lawn again. I watched her race after it.

"And then I have a Council meeting tonight I can't miss."

"What's on the agenda?"

"Christmas decorations. Christmas carnival. Christmas meal delivery for shut-ins. Christmas snowplowing schedule."

"I'm sensing a theme," I said. "Who's playing Santa at the carnival this year?"

"Jackson. Well, at least that was the plan. I guess we'll see if he's up to it."

"Promise to leave enough cookies out, and you can probably convince Josie to do it," I said, laughing.

Too bad she wasn't around to hear it. It was a good one.

Then I remembered I was talking with the woman who pretty much knew everything that was going on in town.

"Have you heard anything about the murder?" I said.

"Not much," she said. "Other than everybody thinks that the owner in Florida is crazy for doing that stupid renovation. I thought the boat was perfect."

"Who is the owner?" I said.

I can't believe this was the first time I had asked that question.

"I think he's in sugar," she said. "Or something like that. But apparently, he's very rich, very eccentric, and very anxious to retire so he can spend the next year on a boat. Can you imagine doing that?"

"No," I said.

I couldn't. As much as I love being on the River, I need to live on land due to the limited number of dogs I can get on a boat. Plus, the idea of eating canned food for an extended period wasn't even worth discussing.

Yeah, I know. When it comes to dogs and food, I'm completely spoiled.

"What a horrible thought," my mother said, shaking her head. "I'd rather be forced to drive a Chevy."

"I drive a Chevy, Mom," I said, glancing at my dirty SUV parked in the driveway.

"So I've noticed, darling," she said as she leaned in to kiss my cheek. "I'll see you Saturday. And when you meet Dirk, remember to play nice."

"Dirk? You're dating a man named Dirk?"

"Yes, Dirk Sinclair," she said, smiling. "Maybe you've heard the name."

I shook my head.

"No, I'm sure I would have remembered that one, Mom."

She waved goodbye and climbed into her car. Chloe and I watched her tear out of the parking lot and disappear down the road.

I glanced down at Chloe who had dropped the tennis ball at my feet. I leaned down and scratched her head and picked the ball up.

"Who the heck names their kid Dirk?" I asked Chloe.

She cocked her head then I watched her effortless strides as she raced after the tennis ball.

I huffed and puffed my way toward the lawn.

Yeah, I know.

I need to get to the gym.

Don't remind me.

Chapter 16

"Your mother thinks she found a keeper?"

"That's what she says."

Josie leaned forward to place a dog biscuit directly in front of Sluggo who was sprawled out at her feet. He sniffed at it, then ignored it and closed his eyes.

"He's still not eating," Josie said. "And those are his favorites."

"Are you sure there's nothing wrong with him?"

Josie looked at me and raised an eyebrow.

"Never mind," I said, knowing that if something had been wrong with Sluggo, she would have found and fixed it already. "Forget I even asked."

"Who's the guy?"

"According to my mom, he owns a foreign car dealership."

"Well, when in Rome, right?" she said, laughing.

"Yeah, I guess," I said. "But with a name like *Dirk Sinclair*, I would have expected him to come straight from the cover of a romance novel."

"She's dating a guy named Dirk?" Josie said.

"Yeah."

"Who the heck names their kid Dirk?"

"That's what I asked Chloe," I said.

"What was her take on it?"

"I couldn't understand what she was saying," I said.

"Still having problems translating dog to English?"

"No, tennis ball in the mouth," I said, laughing.

We heard a knock on the kitchen door, and moments later Chef Claire led Alice into the living room. She appeared distraught, and her eyes were red and puffy.

"Hi," Alice said. "I hope you don't mind me dropping by unannounced. I just had to get out of that motel for a while."

"No problem at all," I said, making room for her on the couch. "Would you like a glass of wine?"

"That would be great," she said, leaning over to pet Chloe who had woken up.

Josie got up to pour a glass for her and refill ours in the process.

"Chef Claire?" Josie said, extending the bottle toward her.

"No, I'm heading out," she said.

"You got a hot date?" I said.

"No, I've got a meeting with a guy who wants to talk to me about running one of his restaurants in Florida."

My stomach dropped, and I was sure that my heart skipped a couple of beats. I looked at Josie. She was in even worse shape than I was.

"Florida?" Josie finally managed to get out.

"Yeah," Chef Claire said. "I was hoping I could figure out a way to open my own place, but at least it's warm down there, right?"

"Warm weather is highly overrated," Josie said.

"Yes, and with all the climate change going on, melanoma has to be on the rise," I said.

"Nice try, guys," Chef Claire said, laughing. "But don't worry. You'll be the first ones to know if I decide to take it."

"For some reason, that doesn't make me feel any better," Josie said.

"I made some snacks. They're in the fridge," Chef Claire said, waving goodbye.

We waited until we heard the door close and then Josie and I stared at each other.

"This can't be happening," I said.

"She certainly knows how to put a damper on the evening," Josie said.

"Well, at least she made snacks."

"She's such a tease," Josie said. "This is horrible news."

I nodded. Devastated by the news, I forced myself to focus on the more pressing concern of what was bothering Alice. I glanced at her, and she took a sip of wine as she continued to rub Chloe's head draped across her lap.

"How are the renovations going?" I said, deciding to ease into the conversation.

"They're getting there," Alice said. "I just wish they'd hurry up and get it done."

"Have they found the other four they were looking for?" I said.

Alice gave me the same alien stare I'd gotten from John.

"What?"

"John mentioned that he was looking for four more workers so they could finish faster," I said.

"Oh," Alice said. "That's news to me. But I'm all for it."

She stared into the fireplace and took a sip of wine.

"So what's gotten you so upset?" Josie said.

"Men. What else would it be?" Alice said, shaking her head.

For one, the possibility of Chef Claire leaving town was pretty high on the list at the moment. But I remained quiet on that front.

"Captain Bill, right?" I said, deciding just to toss it out there and see where the conversation went.

"Oh, the Captain. Him I can handle," Alice said, managing a soft chuckle. "He tries to come across as the daring manly man of the sea, but he's pretty harmless. And he's a follower."

"I see," I said, glancing at Josie. "So who's making your life miserable?"

"I am," she said, laughing. "It's all me."

"No, I meant who's the man-"

"I know what you meant, Suzy," Alice snapped, then immediately softened. "I'm sorry. That was uncalled for."

"Don't worry about it," I said.

She leaned forward and seemed about ready to speak, then she sat back and sighed.

"Jackson will be here Saturday night, right?"

"Yes, he will," I said.

"Good," Alice said. "I need to talk with him."

I glanced at Josie. Apparently, her assumptions about Alice and Jackson were right on the mark. And whatever Jackson had said or done to her had left a scar. Alice seemed to be on the verge of tears again, and Chloe sensed her discomfort and started licking her hand.

"We're just getting ready to start watching a WIJ. You want to join us?" Josie said.

"What's a WIJ?" Alice said, frowning.

"It's a movie. A woman in jeopardy movie. The one tonight is about a woman who has done something terrible and is trying to figure out a way to tell the right people before something really bad happens to her."

"It sounds a little too much like reality," Alice said, getting up from the couch.

"You don't need to leave," I said. "Maybe we can find a comedy."

"No, I should go," Alice said. "I think I need to be alone for a while. But thanks for the wine."

"No problem," Josie said. "Stop by anytime."

"Thanks," she said. "And I'll see you Saturday night."

"Looking forward to it," I said, walking her to the door. "Take care of yourself, Alice."

"Oh, I'm trying," she said, waving over her shoulder on the way out.

I headed for the fridge and removed the tray of snacks. I headed back into the living room and found Josie sprawled out on the couch with an arm draped over her eyes.

"I can't believe it," Josie said.

"What?"

"We're losing her."

"Maybe she'll turn it down," I said.

"We need a plan," Josie said.

"Or a miracle," I said.

"What's that?" she said, sitting up upon noticing the tray covered with aluminum foil.

"Let's have a look," I said, pulling back the foil.

"Is that what I think it is?"

"Yup. Two dozen Cannoli," I said.

"I think I'm gonna cry."

"Just don't do it over the tray. You remember what happened the last time they got wet."

"Suzy?"

"Yes," I said, chuckling.

"Shut up."

Chapter 17

I was standing behind the reception desk chatting with the new owner of a gorgeous pair of spaniel lab mix two-year-olds that were inseparable. We'd had the pair for about six months in our rescue program and had decided early on that the pair had to go to the same home. It had taken a while to find the right family, but looking down at the owner's five-year-old twins rolling around on the tile floor with their two new family members convinced me that we'd made the right decision not to break the dogs up. I asked Sammy to help them into get settled into their car outside and waved goodbye.

"Nice family," Jill said, watching their departure. "We did a good job with those two."

"Yes, we did," I said. "But I'm going to miss having them around."

I leaned over her shoulder to review the morning schedule displayed on her computer screen, and then I caught a glimpse of Chef Claire poking her head around the corner of the entrance to the condo area.

"There you are," Chef Claire said.

"Hey, what's up?" I said. "And thanks for the cannoli."

"No problem," Chef Claire said. "Thanks for saving a couple for me."

"Trust me, it wasn't easy," I said, laughing. "I had to convince Josie that she miscounted."

Then I noticed Josie hovering right behind her, and I knew what Chef Claire wanted to discuss. The party menu had been top of mind for her since we first discussed it. I headed for my office, nodding for both of them to follow. I sat down on the couch, and Chloe hopped onto my lap and stretched out.

"Don't you have other important things you should be doing?" I said to Josie, laughing.

"Not until ten," Josie said, glancing up at the clock on the wall. "And at the moment, nothing is more important than this."

Chef Claire laughed and removed some papers from her jacket.

"You two are unbelievable," she said, shaking her head.

"We like to think so," I said.

"Before we go over the menu, I need to understand something," Chef Claire said, glancing back and forth at us.

"Sure," I said, shrugging.

"What's up with the staggered serving times?" Chef Claire said.

I looked at Josie who took several seconds to think about the question then gestured for me to answer.

"We need to create some subterfuge," I said.

"Okay," Chef Claire said, frowning. "And you thought my Gorgonzola stuffed burgers with pickled coleslaw and fried onions would do the trick?"

"Oh, I was so hoping they'd be on the menu," Josie said.

I felt the same way. The burgers were total knee bucklers.

But for the moment, the burgers were irrelevant.

At least as much as Gorgonzola stuffed burgers with pickled slaw and fried onions could ever be considered irrelevant.

"Josie and I need to disappear from the party for a while, and we need to make sure that everyone who might want to know where we've gone is at our house while we're gone."

"And you thought that if I put together a menu where different dishes were ready at different times that would be the best way to make sure nobody leaves the party early?" Chef Claire said.

"Yeah," Josie said. "Brilliant, huh?"

"Actually, it's not a bad plan," Chef Claire said. "A little nuts maybe, but I'm getting used to that. It's got something to do with the murder and that boat, doesn't it?"

"Yes," I said, nodding.

"You're going snooping," she said.

"Yes," I said. "Probably around 8:30. It'll be completely dark by that time. We should be back by ten at the latest."

Chef Claire frowned.

"What do I tell people if they ask where you've gone?"

"Dog emergency," Josie said.

"I'm impressed," Chef Claire said. "It sounds like you guys have a real plan."

"You seem surprised," I said.

"I was going to say astonished," she said, laughing. "But what the heck, let's go with surprised."

She handed each of us a sheet of paper. Josie and I stared at it. Then we looked up and stared at each other.

"This is amazing," Josie said.

"Yeah, it should be good," Chef Claire said. "But I realized this morning that I'm going to be a couple of warming trays short. You think John might be willing to let us borrow some for the party?"

"I'm sure he will," I said. "And I need to swing by to see him today, so I'll grab them while I'm there."

"You do?" Josie said, giving me a blank stare.

"Yes, I do."

Actually, I didn't. But it was a great excuse to stop by for a chat and perhaps do a bit of snooping.

Chef Claire studied the piece of paper in her hand.

"This is a lot of the items I've always planned to include on the menu when I open my own place." Then she coughed nervously. "And since this might be the last time I cook for you guys, I wanted it to be special. You've been so good to me."

Chef Claire looked out the window and her comment about it being the last time she cooked for us seemed to echo inside my head. Josie was devastated and slumped further down in her chair.

"I take it your meeting last night went well," I finally managed to whisper.

"Yes, it did," Chef Claire said. "It's not a perfect deal by any means, but it's not bad."

"If you accept the offer, when would you start?" I said.

"A week," she said. "Maybe two."

"No," Josie whispered.

Chef Claire broke the somber mood by tapping her fingers rapidly on the desktop.

"You guys will be fine," she said. "And you can always come visit me in Florida." She refocused on the menu. "Okay, if you're going to be gone for an hour and a half, why don't I serve the herb crusted salmon around nine, and the crab-stuffed lobster tails just before ten? That way Suzy will be able to avoid both of the seafood dishes."

Since I detest eating any and all things that come out of the water, I loved the idea.

"Could you serve the salmon around 8:30?" Josie said.

"Sure," Chef Claire said.

"Great," Josie said. "That way I'll be able to grab one to eat on the road."

"Not in my car you won't," I said, shaking my head.

"Then I'll eat it standing *outside* the car before we leave," Josie said, glaring at me. Then she turned to Chef Claire. "And if we don't make it back by ten, save a couple of the lobster tails for me."

"You got it," Chef Claire said, getting up out of her chair. "I need to head into town to start shopping. I'll make the adjustments to the times and review them with you tonight, okay?"

We both sat in silence. I managed a small nod of my head.

"Look, guys," Chef Claire said. "I don't know how to thank you for all you've done for me."

"Stop," I said, holding up a hand. "We are not having this conversation. At least not yet."

"Okay, sure. I get it," Chef Claire whispered. She smiled and gave us a quick goodbye wave then left the office.

"We've lost her," Josie said.

"No, not yet we haven't."

Josie pulled herself out of her chair.

"I need to get to my ten o'clock," she said. "Try not to do anything silly today when you see John."

"I'll do my best," I said, grabbing Chloe's leash, more out of habit than any other reason. She rarely needed it. But she heard the jangle of metal tags, hopped off the couch, and sat waiting by the door. Josie glanced down at Chloe, then back at me.

"You know, you could learn a lot from her," she said.

Her laughter continued to reverberate down the hallway long after she'd left the office.

Chloe and I headed into town, and I parked in front of John's office. I climbed out of the car and noticed Captain Bill climbing down the stairway of the yacht onto the dock. He saw me and waved. I returned the wave and decided to wait. He approached, said hello, and knelt down to pet Chloe.

"How are the renovations going?" I said.

"If they don't hurry up, we're going to need an ice boat to get out of here."

It was a total exaggeration, but I understood where he was coming from. The temperature had continued to drop, and a brisk wind out of the north made it seem at least ten degrees colder. I zipped my jacket up and bounced up and down on my tiptoes for warmth.

It was a very brief workout, but I'm counting it.

"How much longer do they think they're going to need?" I said.

"They say if they get lucky, maybe they'll finish over the weekend," Captain Bill said.

"Lucky?"

"They're a bit stuck at the moment," he said, giving Chloe one last head rub and standing up.

"Another math problem?" I said, remembering John's comment from the end of summer party.

"What?" Captain Bill said, frowning.

"John mentioned something about a math problem," I said.

I had touched a nerve, and I studied his reaction closely.

"Did he now? Well, John's always going on about something, isn't he?"

"Yeah, I guess," I said. "Are you still planning on coming to the party?"

"I wouldn't miss it," he said, giving me an odd smile that seemed to say he knew something I didn't.

"How's Alice doing?"

I figured that since I had gotten his attention, I'd push him a bit.

"She's anxious to get this show on the road. Just like me," he said, staring out at the water.

"That's a long time to be on a boat," I said. "I don't know how you can deal with it."

"Oh, I'm sure we'll find plenty of ways to kill time," he said, winking at me.

The wink hit about an eight on the creep-factor scale. I forced a smile and stuffed my hands in my pockets.

"Have you seen John?"

"He's not on the boat, so I guess he's in his office," Captain Bill said.

"Thanks. Well, I'll see you Saturday," I said.

"I'm looking forward to it. I'm just heading over to the Water's Edge for a drink. You feeling like joining me?" he said, staring at me.

Thankfully, he didn't wink again.

"No, thanks," I said. "I have a policy against drinking before lunch."

"Actually, it won't be *before* lunch. It will *be* lunch. Just one of the liquid variety," he said, laughing hard and loud.

It was hard to argue with that kind of logic, so I didn't even bother to try. I waved goodbye and headed for John's office. I found him behind his desk chatting with Alice who was sitting on the couch. She continued to look worn out.

"Hey, Suzy," John said, beaming at me. "We were just talking about you."

"I seriously doubt that," I said, sitting down on the couch next to Alice and patting her knee.

"Hi, Suzy," she said. "Actually we were just talking about what might be on the menu for Saturday night."

"I just went over it with Chef Claire," I said. "You're going to love it."

"You didn't happen to see Captain Bill on your way in, did you?" John said.

"Yes, I did," I said, nodding. "He just headed for the Water's Edge. He mentioned something about having a liquid lunch."

"Geez, here we go again," John said, glancing at Alice. "You better get over there and keep an eye on him."

"This is getting old," Alice said, getting up off the couch.

"Hang in there," John said. "You'll be on your way soon on an adventure of a lifetime."

"Yeah, a month on a boat with him and the copulating Canadians. Gee, John, why doesn't that make me feel better?"

She glared at him.

"Relax, Alice," John said softly. "You need to dial it down a bit. Just head over the Water's Edge and try to keep him under one bottle of scotch. Grab some lunch and enjoy the afternoon. Just tell Millie to put it on my tab."

"Fine," Alice said, storming out of the office.

John glanced at me and shook his head.

"Everybody is a bit on edge," he said. "Alice thought she'd be on the water by now and it's never a good thing when Captain Bill has too much free time on his hands."

"Maybe he needs a hobby," I said.

"He has one," John said, laughing.

"Drinking's not a hobby," I said, laughing along.

"No, you're probably right. Captain Bill has managed to elevate it to an art form."

"Is Alice going to be okay?"

"She'll be fine. I think she's having some relationship problems," John said.

"Really? Do tell," I said, leaning forward and beaming at him.

"I have no idea who it is," he said. "But Alice is young, and I guess this is the first time she's had her heart broken." He seamlessly changed topics. "So what brings you by?"

"I need a small favor. Chef Claire needs a few more of warming trays for the party. I was wondering if we could borrow some of yours."

"Sure. Not a problem."

He punched a number on his phone and seconds later we heard a voice on the other end.

"Maintenance."

"Hey, Bill."

"What's up, John?"

"Suzy Chandler is here, and she needs to borrow some of our warming trays. Would you mind grabbing some and putting them in the back of her car?"

"You got it."

"Are you driving your SUV today?" John asked me.

"Yes. It's parked right in front, and it's not locked," I said loud enough to be heard through the phone. "Thanks, Bill. Four should be plenty."

"You got it, Suzy. And I'll see you Saturday."

He ended the call, and I glanced around the office. I stopped when I saw the shotgun displayed on the wall behind the desk. I'd been in the office at least a dozen times and couldn't remember ever seeing it before.

"While you're waiting, let's go for a walk down to the boat," John said, standing up. "How about you Chloe? Feel like taking a look at the boat?"

Chloe was apparently up for anything today. She hopped off my lap and raced to the door. She sat down and wagged her tail.

"That dog is scary smart," John said, laughing.

"She gets it from her mother," I said, nodding my head at the wall. "That's a nice shotgun. Is that new?"

"No, I've had that forever," he said. "But I don't use it to hunt anymore, and I thought it might look good on the wall."

"And it's probably a good reminder to the staff not to mess with you," I said, following him out the door.

"Oh, I don't think they need any reminders," he said, laughing as he held the door open for me.

The wind hit us full bore when we stepped outside. It even got Chloe's attention and she stared up at me and barked once when he headed away from where the car was parked.

At the edge of the stairway, John scooped Chloe up in his arms and carried her up the stairs. I could have probably managed to get up the stairs without dropping her into the water, but I was glad I didn't have to try.

Near the bow, I saw one of the renovation crew working on a latch that was attached to what looked like a storage area directly in front of the wheelhouse. Judging by how hard he was hitting it with a hammer, he wasn't very happy with the way it was working.

I wondered if wheelhouse was the right term to use for a yacht this size. Or was it called the bridge? Or maybe it was the Captain's Chair? Whatever they called it, it was the spot from where the person who piloted the boat was situated.

I followed John below deck and stepped into the newly renovated area. Long gone was the marble and wood now replaced by some form of composite material I thought looked dreadful. But since it wasn't my boat or my money, and if the owner in Florida wanted a yacht whose interior looked like a lunch counter you might find in a mini-mall, who was I to judge.

"How are you doing?" John said to the supervisor.

"We're getting there, John. Two down, two to go," the supervisor said.

I glanced around but didn't see the two extra workers. Maybe they were at lunch. I hoped for John sake that they weren't at the Water's Edge having

105

lunch with Captain Bill. That would probably put a serious dent in the afternoon productivity.

"Have you sent the owner photos of how this looks?" I said to John.

"Yeah," he said, shaking his head. "The guy loves it."

"Really?" I said, finding that impossible to believe.

"Yeah. I hate it, too. But you need to remember one important fact," John said. "The guy's an idiot."

I nodded and then moved out of the way as the man who had been hammering on the latch on the top deck, strode past me into the master stateroom. Soon I heard the hammering start again.

"What's the deal with all the hammering?" I said.

"Just one more change the guy wants," John said, closing the door that led into the stateroom. "He didn't like the way the gold latches looked. Now he wants silver."

"He sounds incredibly picky," I said.

"Trust me," John said. "The guy who owns this boat knows exactly what he wants, but sometimes he feels compelled to change his mind. The trick is to get it right and delivered before something else happens."

"I'm so glad I do what I do," I said. "Dogs ask for so little, and they're always satisfied."

"You're a very lucky woman, Suzy."

He's right.

I am.

And as far as solving this case went, that was a good thing.

It was beginning to look like I was going to need every bit of luck I could find.

Chapter 18

On a whim, and out of ideas, I called Josie at the Inn and asked her if she'd like to meet me for lunch at the Water's Edge. Since their burgers and French fries were one of her favorites, she quickly agreed and told me she'd meet me there in twenty minutes.

The Water's Edge was only about two hundred yards from where I was parked, and I stood next to the driver's door and thought about walking.

No, don't laugh. I did consider it.

But when I ran the pros and cons through my head, the decision to walk was anything but automatic. I knew the exercise would do me good, but after lunch, I'd have to walk back into a stiff north wind on a full stomach. Eventually, the cons won out, and I opened the door, waited for Chloe to hop into the passenger seat, then got in and drove up the street.

The Water's Edge, unlike most of the bars and restaurants that close at the end of summer, is open year round and a favorite with the locals. It was more bar than restaurant, but the place was welcoming, and the food was great. It was also dog-friendly.

I held the door open for Chloe, who trotted inside like she owned the place and waited for me to make up my mind about where to sit. I glanced around and waved at two locals who were watching afternoon baseball on the TV above the bar and drinking draft beer. At a table in the back, I saw Alice and Captain Bill. They both gave me a quick wave and then went back to what they'd been doing. Alice was eating a burger while it looked like Captain Bill was doing shots and a lot of arm waving.

I selected a table a safe distance away from them and sat down. Chloe stared up at me while I studied the menu. Laughing, I set the menu down and rubbed her head.

"Don't worry," I said to Chloe. "You'll get your burger."

That seemed to satisfy her, and she stretched out over my feet under the table. She stayed there for about a minute before the owner's German Shepherd wandered over and nudged Chloe with his nose. They checked each other, seemed satisfied, and then the German shepherd turned his attention to me. We were old friends, and I gave him a big hug.

"Hey, Barkley," I said. "How are you doing?" I glanced up as Millie, the owner of both the dog and the Water's Edge, approached. "Hey, Millie."

"Hi, Suzy," she said kneeling down to pet Chloe. "Barkley, please don't do that. I'm sorry about that."

"Don't worry about it. It happens all the time." Laughing, I gently removed Barkley's head from my lap.

"Are you eating by yourself today?"

"No, Josie's on her way," I said.

"So is your mother," Millie said.

"What?"

"Yeah, she just called to make sure I had clam chowder as one of the specials today. She's bringing someone she said was her *very special friend*."

"Don't you have a chef's table in the kitchen?" I said.

"Not a chance," she said, laughing.

"That's too bad," I said, fending off the German shepherd's attempt to find out what was in my coat pocket. "I'd ask you to seat my mother as far away as possible, but we both know she's going to sit wherever she wants to."

"She's going to sit with you and Josie, and you know it," Millie said.

"Maybe there's still time for me to slip out the back," I said.

"You're terrible," Millie said, shaking her head. "You ready to order?"

"Sure," I said. "Two burgers with extra fries on both plates. And a small burger with no bun and no seasoning for Chloe, please."

"You got it," Millie said. "What would you like to drink?"

"What do you have on tap at the moment? I haven't had a beer in a long time."

"We've got a nice pilsner from a microbrewery in the Finger Lakes that's really good," she said.

"Sounds good. Two of those. Thanks."

"You got it," she said, snapping her fingers once in her dog's direction. "Let's go, Barkley. It's time for you to terrorize somebody else. Like the dishwasher."

Millie headed toward the kitchen with the dog at her heels. Moments later, Josie entered and waited for her eyes to adjust to the dim light. Then she saw me and headed for the table. The two men watching baseball took a break from the action to watch Josie until she'd settled into her chair. If Josie had even noticed their leering, she didn't let on. She'd changed out of her scrubs into jeans and a baggy wool sweater and sneakers. Her long hair was tied back and trailed down her back. She looked like she could have spent an hour getting ready. My guess was a minute and a half tops. Chloe climbed out from under the table and placed her front paws on Josie's lap.

"Did you order?" Josie said, petting Chloe.

"Yeah, burger, extra fries. And I ordered you a beer."

"Oh, good call," she said. "I haven't one in a long time. Is that Alice and Captain Bill in the back?"

"It is indeed," I said.

I gave her the summary version of my morning, and she listened closely. She sat back when Millie delivered our beers and exchanged pleasantries with Josie. After she had left, Josie leaned forward.

"So Captain Bill is an alcoholic?" Josie said.

"It certainly sounds that way," I said.

"I guess there's not a lot to do out there on the open water, huh?"

We each took a sip of beer and nodded our approval.

"Alice seems to be even more on edge," I said.

"Do you really think it was Jackson who broke her heart?" she said, sneaking a peek over her shoulder.

"I don't know who else it could be," I said.

"And you're going to ask him about it, right?"

"Of course," I said.

She laughed.

"Welcome home, Jackson. It's so good to see you. Now would you care to explain why you felt the need to break that young woman's heart?"

"I'll be more subtle than that, and you know it," I said.

Josie snorted but cut it short. She stared at the entrance.

"What is it?"

"Here comes the floor show," Josie said.

"Great."

"Darling, what a wonderful surprise," my mother called out. "Hi, Josie."

"Hi Mrs. C," Josie said, waving.

I turned around and saw my mother approaching. For her, she was dressed down. Boots, jeans, sweater, and a leather coat that probably cost more than my car. But what got my full attention was the fact that she was holding hands with the man walking next to her. I was shocked. My mother was very comfortable doing many things in public that attracted attention to her. But holding hands wasn't one of them. At least it never had been.

"Darling, I'd like you to meet Dirk Sinclair," she gushed. "Dirk, this is my beautiful daughter, Suzy."

I accepted his handshake and smiled up at him.

"It's nice to meet you, Suzy," he said, flashing me a wide grin that displayed what I assumed were some very expensive teeth. "Your mother has told me so much about you."

"Yeah, well, I wouldn't put too much stock in that. She's a drinker."

He laughed loudly, just the way I would have expected someone who sold cars for a living to laugh, then he got his first look at Josie. He flinched like he'd just put his hand on a hot stove or maybe a finger in a light socket, but quickly recovered.

"It's *so* nice to meet you, Josie," he said, extending his hand across the table.

"Same here," Josie said, forcing a smile. "Should I call you *Dirk*?"

"Of course," he said, gushing.

I smiled and looked down at the table. I knew Josie better than anyone, and I already knew the word she would later use to describe Dirk Sinclair.

And that word was smarmy.

"Didn't I tell you they were both beautiful?" my mother said.

"Yes, you did," Dirk Sinclair said. "And they certainly are."

I was guessing Dirk had already forgotten what I looked like since he was unable to stop staring at Josie. I started silently counting down from ten in my head.

Nine… eight.

If Dirk Sinclair knew what was good for him, he would soon refocus his attention on the woman sitting across the table from him.

Seven… six.

My mother's eyes started to glaze over.

Five... four.

She rotated her head sideways until one of her neck vertebrae emitted a soft pop.

C'mon, Dirk. Get your act together. I haven't had my burger yet, and I don't want a major incident before I get a chance to eat.

Three... two.

Earth to Dirk.

"Of course, with all due respect, they both pale in comparison to you, my dear," Dirk Sinclair said, looking at my mother and reaching across the table to squeeze her hand.

"Oh, you're so sweet, Dirkie," my mother said.

"Dirkie?" Josie whispered.

I stifled a laugh but had to admit that he'd managed to pull out of his nosedive.

Well done. Nice save. Score a point for Dirk.

"So I hear you're in cars," I said.

"Yes, mainly," he said, sitting back in his chair to take command of the table. "And the next time you two ladies are thinking about a new car, you must come see me." His eyes strayed back to Josie. "I'd just love to get you behind the wheel of a Mercedes."

At least that's what came out of his mouth. I knew that what he was actually thinking was that he'd love to get Josie in the *backseat* of a Mercedes.

"Yeah, cars have been very good to me," Dirk Sinclair said. "But lately, I've started to get into restaurants."

"Really?" I said, nodding my head.

I was about as interested in that fact as I was in who was winning the baseball game.

"Yes," he said. "In fact, last night I met with a young chef about running one of my restaurants in Florida."

"What?" I said, suddenly a lot more interested in what Dirk Sinclair was saying.

I grabbed the sides of my chair with both hands to stop myself from grabbing him by the throat. I looked across the table at Josie who was squeezing her fork. Then the fork literally folded in half. Josie glanced down at it in her hand, then set it down and pushed it away. I casually reached across the table and pulled her knife toward me. I moved it a safe distance away then looked at Josie who was giving Dirk Sinclair the death stare.

"That's interesting news," my mother said. "Who is it?"

"She goes by the name Chef Claire," he said. "Apparently, her food is amazing."

"Chef Claire?" my mother whispered.

"Yes, do you know her?" Dirk Sinclair said.

"Why, yes. As a matter of fact I do," my mother said.

I'm not sure if she knew it or not, but my mother was about to be facing a major decision. She might be in love, but this guy was messing around with our ability to eat great food.

"Is her food as good as everyone says?" he said.

"Well," my mother said, glancing back and forth at Josie and me. "What do you girls have to say about Chef Claire's food?"

"I guess it's okay," Josie said, shrugging.

"Yeah, I'd say fair to middling," I said, unable to maintain eye contact. "Oh, great. Our lunch is here,"

We all sat back as Millie arranged our plates in front of us. She made sure we were all set and then headed back to the kitchen. I cut Chloe's burger into small pieces and set it down on the floor. I waited for her to get started and then focused on my lunch.

Rule number one; feed your animals first.

I picked up my burger, then stopped and looked across the table when a thought popped into my head.

"Hey, wait a minute. You didn't even order," I said to my mother.

"I called it in earlier, darling," my mother said, dipping her spoon into a bowl of clam chowder.

She was having trouble maintaining eye contact as well. I knew she knew that if Chef Claire left to go work for her new boyfriend, Dirk Sinclair would forever remain on Josie's and my list of the most hated people in the world. But for now, it appeared to be a risk my mother thought was worth taking. She reached across the table and held one of his hands while she spooned clam chowder into her mouth with the other.

I looked at Josie, and we both stared at the chowder-fueled love fest playing out in front of us.

We ate lunch in relative silence, and Dirk Sinclair *simply insisted* on picking up the check. We thanked him and got ready to leave.

"So, I guess we'll see you Saturday night," my mother said, going for a lighthearted tone.

I glared at her. Josie scanned the table, ostensibly for her keys. Personally, I think she was looking for the knife.

"Should we bring anything?" my mother said, forcing a smile at me.

"No, I think we're all set. We'll have tons of food, some music, a full bar," I said.

"Your death certificates," Josie whispered.

"What was that, Josie?" my mother said.

"Nothing, Mrs. C," she said, flashing my mother a quick smile.

"Well, it was certainly nice to finally meet you, Suzy," Dirk Sinclair said.

"Yeah, same here," I managed to get out.

And then he spread his arms wide. I stared at them and then looked at him.

"Too soon for a hug?" he said.

"Absolutely," I said, extending my hand.

"It was great meeting you, too, Josie," he said, extending his hand toward Josie.

She stared at his hand, then shared a brief handshake with him.

"See you around, *Dirk*," Josie said, zipping her jacket.

"This was wonderful," my mother gushed. "And I think it's only the first of hundreds of wonderful meals we'll be sharing together."

I glared at my mother. Without actually having to come out and say it to my face, she was telling me that she had made her choice.

I nodded, and then Josie and I headed for the door with Chloe leading the way.

Okay, Mom. Have it your way.

Game on.

Chapter 19

If our lunch with my mother and her smarmy, chef-stealing scoundrel for a boyfriend could be considered quiet, dinner was like watching a silent movie in a morgue. At least that's how Freddie, our local medical examiner, described it.

I had to agree with him. It looked like we were going to make it through the entire meal in total silence, which would be a first. The mood in the kitchen was tense with everyone afraid to speak and run the risk of waking the eight-hundred-pound elephant in the room.

Or maybe since the loss of Chef Claire and her food was the top-of-mind topic, maybe the elephant was in the fridge.

I'd completely forgotten that we had invited Freddie to dinner until he'd knocked on our door at seven sharp. Chef Claire and I ran into him earlier in the week when we were grocery shopping, and she'd mentioned that she was making a roast dinner tonight. When Freddie turned melancholy in Aisle 7 and mentioned how roast dinners always reminded him of Sunday nights with his parents, who were both now deceased, we did what friends do and invited him to join us.

But despite the mushroom and horseradish stuffed beef roast and two trays of perfectly roasted garlic and rosemary vegetables, Freddy could be excused for wondering if he'd made a mistake accepting our invitation. It wasn't anger that filled the kitchen. The mood was more sad than mad, and it reminded me of a frigid, windblown February morning where all you could do was hunker down and try to survive until things started to warm up.

If Freddie had been looking for melancholy, he'd come to the right place.

"So Freddie," I said, desperate to hear anything other than the swordplay of Josie's silverware. "What's going on in your world?"

"Not too much," he said, glancing around the table as if checking first if it was okay for him to respond. "It's been pretty quiet this week. And that's fine with me."

"I'd keep my phone turned on if I were you, Freddie. Things could change in a hurry," Josie said, glancing at Chef Claire.

"Geez, Josie," Chef Claire said. "You'd think I killed a dog. Let it go."

"I can't help it," Josie said. "I feel so betrayed."

"You're unbelievable," Chef Claire said, pushing her plate away.

"It's one thing for you to leave. But how could you leave to go work for that smarmy creature? I had to take a shower when I got home from lunch today."

That was true. She did. But not because of anything Dirk Sinclair had done. Josie had been so upset by the news about Chef Claire she'd lost focus at lunch and had ended up with burger juice up and down both arms and a handful of ketchup-soaked French fries inside her sweater.

I was still trying to understand the science of how she managed to pull that off.

"How could you do that?" Josie repeated.

"Because it's the only job offer I have at the moment and winter is fast approaching," Chef Claire said, getting up from the table to remove a chocolate chip cheesecake from the fridge.

"What job are you talking about?" Freddie said.

"I'm going to Florida to be head chef and manager of a restaurant outside of Orlando," Chef Claire said, cutting a large wedge of cheesecake and sliding it in front of Josie.

It didn't solve her problem with Josie, but it was a good start.

"Good for you. That's great," Freddie said, digging into his dessert.

"Are you out of your mind?" Josie said, glaring at Freddie.

"What?"

"What's great about it?" Josie said, maintaining her stare.

"I don't know," he said, shrugging. "Maybe because she's a chef who likes warm weather and it sounds like a great opportunity. I would have thought you'd be happy for her as a friend instead of being so selfish."

Wow. I'm not sure I'd give Freddie any points for knowing when to keep one's mouth shut, but I had to admire his courage.

"What did you call me?" Josie said.

Freddie stared back at her and maintained eye contact even as her glare narrowed and turned dark.

"I called you selfish," Freddie said. "Why don't you try to stop thinking about your stomach for five minutes and start thinking about what's best for one of your good friends?"

"Nobody ever talks to me like that," Josie said.

"Well, maybe it's time somebody started," Freddie snapped.

I watched the death stare play itself out and almost laughed when I considered the irony wrapped up in the problem of trying to find someone to perform the examination of the body if our local ME got killed in our kitchen.

Josie slowly chewed a mouthful of cheesecake and stared off into the distance. Eventually, she did what she always did. She set her fork down and looked at Freddie.

"You're right," she said, nodding her head. "I'm being selfish. I'm sorry."

"Don't worry about it," he said, taking another bite of cheesecake. "It happens."

Josie stood and hugged Chef Claire.

"I'm sorry," Josie said. "It's just that I'm going to miss you so much."

"I know," Chef Claire said as she patted Josie's back. "And?"

Josie sighed.

"Okay, maybe I'm also going to miss your food a bit," Josie said, sitting down to resume her attack on the cheesecake.

Chef Claire laughed and gave Josie another brief hug before sitting down at the table.

"So tell me all about this new restaurant," Freddie said.

"Don't push your luck, Freddie," Josie snapped.

Another round of tense silence followed before Josie burst out laughing. I shook my head at her and helped myself to a second slice.

"The restaurant's okay," Chef Claire said. "From the photos, it looks a little rundown, and the menu needs a total makeover, but Dirk said he's willing to put the money into it."

"Dirk Sinclair?" Freddie said.

"Yes," Chef Claire said. "Do you know him?"

"A little," Freddie said. "I bought my last car at his dealership. And I just saw him the other day when I was downriver. He was having lunch with who I assumed was his girlfriend. They were all over each other in the restaurant."

"You mean my mother, right?" I said.

"What does your mother have to do with this?" Freddie said, frowning at me.

"It wasn't my mother who was with him?" I said.

"Suzy, I've known your mother for over a decade. If she had been there, I think I would have recognized her."

"So who was he with?" Josie said.

"Some hot young blonde in her twenties," Freddie said, refocusing on his cheesecake. "Good looking with big, well, I could probably go on, but I think you get the drift."

"Yeah, we got it," I said.

"Your mom is going to be devastated," Josie said.

"Yeah, she is. We need to tell her," I said.

"There you go again with that collective *we* thing," Josie said, laughing. "Nice try."

"You're right, I need to tell her," I said. "How the heck do I do that?"

"Very slowly and from a safe distance," Josie said.

My mom and I may argue and battle with each other on a regular basis, but we would run through fire for each other if necessary. And unless *Dirk* and my mother had an understanding about dating other people, he'd crossed the line with this one.

Nobody messes with my mom.

"Dirk's about to experience a world of hurt," I said.

"It couldn't happen to a nicer guy," Josie said.

"I thought you decided to let it go," Chef Claire said.

"With you, yes," Josie said. "Him, forget it. He's managed to steal you away, and now he's messing with Suzy's mom. And because of him, I ended up with French fries in my bra."

"What?" Freddie said, perking up immediately.

"It's a long story," Josie said.

"I've got time," Freddie said.

It turned out Freddie didn't have time because his phone started buzzing.

"This is Freddie… What? … Geez, I'm right in the middle of cheesecake that's bringing tears to my eyes… Okay. I'll be there in about ten minutes."

Freddie ended the call and slid his phone back into his pocket. He stood up and glanced around the table.

"I need to run."

"What is it?" I said.

"There's a little problem down at John's place. Actually, the problem is at the dock."

"Who is it?" I said.

"Did I say it was a person?" Freddie said.

"I doubt if they'd call you if a tree had fallen in the park," Josie said.

"Yeah, you've got a point there. It's Captain Bill. It looks like he was drinking all day, and for some reason, he decided to go onto the boat."

"And?" I said, glancing at Josie.

"He did a header off the dock and ended up getting wedged between the boat and one of the pilings."

"He's dead?" I said.

"Yes, hence the call," Freddie said.

I stood up and grabbed my car keys.

"Where do you think you're going?" Freddie said.

"To have a look. What else?" I said.

Josie hopped up out of her chair and grabbed her coat.

"If you don't mind, I think I'll just stay here and clean up," Chef Claire said.

"You mind keeping an eye on Chloe and Sluggo?" I said.

"Not a problem," Chef Claire said, giving Freddie a quick hug. "I'll see you Saturday, Freddie."

I waved goodbye and raced out the door with Josie close behind. We climbed into my SUV and managed to beat Freddie to the scene. We spotted John talking quietly with Detective Abrams from the state police at the front of the dock and wandered toward them. Detective Abrams gave us a quick wave then headed down the dock toward the boat. Freddie arrived, parked, and then hustled past us with a quick wave.

"What are you two doing here?" John said.

121

He looked bewildered and completely worn down.

"Freddie was having dinner at our place when the call came in, and we just thought we'd swing by to see if you needed anything."

Despite the gravity of the situation, John glanced back and forth at us and laughed softly.

"You guys are something else," he said.

"We like to think so," I said, forcing a smile. "So Captain Bill fell in and drowned?"

"It looks that way. I just spoke with Millie from the Water's Edge, and she said Captain Bill was so hammered she had to cut him off around five. Then he went to the liquor store and bought a bottle of Scotch. Nobody saw him after that until somebody discovered his body."

"Who found him?" Josie said.

"Gladys Robertson," John said.

"The name sounds familiar," I said, then looked at Josie. "Do we know her?"

"Yeah, she has the two black labs. Dexter and Daisy," Josie said.

"Oh, sure," I said. "She's a nice woman."

"Yeah," Josie said. "And they're great dogs."

"Ladies, please," John said with an edge working its way into his voice. "Mrs. Robertson was walking her dogs when they must have picked up the scent. She said they dragged her down the dock to where the body was."

"That must have been traumatic for her," I said. "And probably the dogs as well."

"Not as traumatic as it must have been for Captain Bill," Josie said.

"Well, sure, that goes without saying," I said

John, out of patience with us, exhaled loudly.

"Look, I would love to stand here and chat, but if you'll excuse me, I have a lot to take care of at the moment."

"Sure, we understand," I said, rocking back and forth on my feet to beat back the cold.

"If you're going to insist on hanging around, please stay away from the scene and let the police and Freddie do their thing."

We both nodded and then John starting to walk down the dock.

"Hey, John," I said.

"What?"

"How's the renovation going?"

"That's the weird thing," he said, walking back toward us. "We should have everything wrapped up on Saturday morning. And if that's the case, the plan is to head out first thing Monday morning. Captain Bill only needed to hang in there a few more days."

"And now you need a new captain," I said.

"Yes, I do," John said. "Unfortunately, I don't have anyone I can find on such short notice, so I'm going to have to do it."

"You?" Josie said.

"Yeah, and in case you can't tell, I'm not very happy about it. There goes my trip down the St. Lawrence to the Atlantic and then to Florida along the coastline."

"Duty calls, huh?" I said.

"Yeah, duty, all my creditors, and my bank," he said, laughing. "Okay, I'll see you Saturday. And do me a favor and try to keep your snooping to a minimum tonight."

"We'll do our best," I said.

"Yes, that's what I'm afraid of."

He waved and headed off.

"I'm beginning to think that boat is cursed," I said.

"Cursed enough to call off our visit on Saturday night?" Josie said, bouncing up and down from the cold.

"You know I can't do that," I said, shivering. "Are you positive it's only September? Man, it is freezing."

"Yeah. Let's get out of here. We'll get the scoop from Freddie tomorrow."

We started walking back to the car.

"Freddie got your attention tonight, didn't he?" I said, opening my door.

"He certainly did. I didn't think he had it in him."

"He was very forceful," I said.

"Yup."

"And intense."

"Yup."

"He got your motor running, didn't he?"

"Maybe."

We drove in silence for a while before Josie glanced over at me.

"We could be in for a long winter."

"It certainly looks that way. Maybe we can figure out a way to get down to Florida," I said.

"I'd rather figure out a way to convince Chef Claire that winter isn't that bad."

"You mean we need to lie to her," I said.

"Desperate times call for desperate measures," Josie said.

"I thought you said you were going to let it go," I said.

"No, what I said was that I was going to respect and accept whatever decision she made. I didn't say I wasn't going to do everything I could to help her change her mind."

"I like the way you think," I said.

"Your mother might be able to help us out," Josie said.

"Definitely. I was thinking the same thing," I said. "We just need to figure out a way to let my mother think it was her idea."

"Are you thinking about a revenge play?"

"I am," I said.

"So what are we going to do?"

"I have no idea," I said, pulling into the driveway.

"You know, whenever I need to think things through," Josie said. "I've always found that a little snack helps to get my brain working."

"Are you thinking maybe a slice of chocolate chip cheesecake?"

"I could eat."

Chapter 20

On Friday afternoon Josie and I, along with Chloe and Sluggo, were waiting at Jackson's house when his father pulled into the driveway. Jackson climbed out of the passenger seat, and Sluggo dashed towards him. This time, the sounds he was making were those of a very happy dog. Jackson knelt down to pet him, wobbled briefly, then stood back up.

"Easy does it, Jackson," Josie said, holding his shoulder to steady him.

"I guess the doctor wasn't joking when he said my balance might be off for a while," Jackson said, reaching down to rub Sluggo's head. "He's lost weight. Have you had him on a diet?"

"He's been off his food while you were away," I said, tossing him a plastic bag of dog biscuits I'd brought with me. "Try giving him one of those. Hey, Mr. Frank. How are you doing?"

Jackson gave the dog one of the biscuits, and it was evident that Sluggo had rediscovered his appetite. He devoured the biscuit and looked up at Jackson for another.

"Hi, Suzy, Josie," Mr. Frank said. "It was nice of you to meet us here."

"We wouldn't have missed it," I said. "Let's get in out of the wind. We brought some ham and spinach soup and fresh bread that Chef Claire made. It's on the stove and ready to go."

"That sounds great," Mr. Frank said.

"It is," Josie said, then caught the look we were giving her. "Relax. I just had a little taste."

We headed inside and sat down in the living room while Jackson, trailed closely by Sluggo, put his things in his bedroom. Mr. Frank sat down across from us. He looked tired but relieved.

"On the drive home, I tried again to convince him to quit being a cop and take over the store," Mr. Frank.

"And?" Josie said.

"No luck. He's so stubborn," Mr. Frank said. "He gets that from his mother in case you were wondering."

"What did he get from you?" Josie said.

"His incredible good looks. What else?"

"He likes being the Chief of Police," I said, laughing.

"I know," Mr. Frank said.

Jackson and Sluggo entered the living room, and Jackson sat down on the couch. Sluggo was soon sprawled over his lap panting contentedly.

"Bad news about Captain Bill, huh? Jackson said. "That's a tough way to go."

"Yeah, it is," I said. "We talked with Freddie yesterday, and he said that the cold weather would probably have sobered him up enough to climb out, but that his body got wedged against one of the pilings. The boat rocking sideways would explain all the body bruises."

"Sure. And the head wound," Jackson said, nodding.

"What head wound?" I said, glancing at Josie.

"He had a big bump on the back of his head," Jackson said.

"Oh, Freddie didn't mention that," I said, glancing at Josie.

"I don't think I like the look on your face, Suzy," Jackson said. "What is it?"

"It's probably nothing," I said. "It's just that you got hit on the back of the head, and Captain Bill also had a head wound. But I'm sure it's just a coincidence."

"Let it go, Suzy," Jackson said, shaking his head.

"What?"

"You know what I'm talking about," Jackson said.

"I just think it's curious," I said. "And we do still have an unsolved murder to worry about."

"Yes, I'm aware of that," Jackson said. "But let me correct you on one thing. *I* have an unsolved murder. *We* don't."

"Ah, the dreaded collective we," Josie whispered.

"What?" Jackson said, glancing at Josie.

"Nothing," Josie said, laughing.

I punched her in the arm and looked at Jackson.

"You have nothing to worry about, Jackson," I said. "Besides, *we* have a party to get ready for, and we're much too busy to help you do your job."

"Thanks. I appreciate that," Jackson deadpanned.

Josie stood up and pulled on her coat.

"Let's go Miss Marples," she said. "We'll see both of you tomorrow night."

We said our goodbyes and climbed into the car.

"Interesting," I said, turning the ignition key.

"No, Suzy. It's not that interesting at all."

"You know what we need to do, right?" I said, backing out of the driveway.

"Well, I'm afraid I know what you need to do," she said, fastening her seat belt.

"How does your afternoon look?"

"I have a surgery scheduled right after lunch," Josie said.

"We've got plenty of time," I said, heading for downtown.

Five minutes later, we found Freddie in his office. He had his feet up on the desk and was reading a medical journal. When we entered, he put the journal down but kept his feet on the desk.

"Why aren't I surprised to see you two here?" he said, grinning.

"We just happened to be in the neighborhood and thought we'd drop in to say hi," I said.

Josie snorted. It truly wasn't one of her better qualities and sometimes it made me cranky. This was one of those times.

"Sure, why not? Let's go with just happened to be in the neighborhood," Freddie said.

"We were just chatting with Jackson," I said.

"Oh, good, he's home. How's he doing?"

"He's fine," I said. "Why didn't you tell us that Captain Bill had a big bump on the back of his head?"

"Because I knew that if I did, you'd come in here and start throwing around a bunch of theories and asking a ton of questions about things that are none of your business," Freddie said.

"Well, I guess your strategy didn't work very well, did it?" I said.

Josie snorted again. I gave her a hard stare that she completely ignored.

"So what can you tell us about the lump on Captain Bill's head?"

"It was big. And lumpy," Freddie deadpanned.

Josie snorted for the third time.

"Will you please stop doing that?" I said, glaring at her.

"What can I tell you? It was funny," Josie said.

"Thanks," Freddie said.

"You're welcome," Josie said.

"How do you think he got the bump?"

Freddie shrugged.

"Look, Suzy, the guy probably had half a distillery in him. Maybe he fell earlier in the day. Maybe he fell on the dock. Or hit the piling when he fell in the water. Or the side of the boat. I don't know, Suzy. It doesn't matter, does it?"

"Could it have been caused by someone hitting him in the head?" I said.

"Sure," Freddie said. "He could have also been hit with a hockey puck, but they don't start playing for another month. For the record, I've already ruled out the hockey puck thing."

This time, Josie laughed. It was better than hearing her snort, but it was still annoying.

"So you're saying that he could have been murdered," I said.

"No, I said no such thing," Freddie said. "I'm saying he fell into the water and drowned."

"But it's possible, right?"

"Unbelievable," Freddie said, shaking his head. "Don't you have a bunch of dogs you need to care of?"

"Freddie, you won't get anywhere trying to play the dog card with me," I said. "Our dogs are just fine, thank you very much."

"Then how about, don't you have a party to get ready for?" Freddie said.

"No, we're pretty much set to go," I said, shaking my head.

"Let me try this then," he said. "What would it take to get you to stop asking questions and go away?"

"Just tell me if it's possible that someone hit Captain Bill in the head before he went in the water."

"Yes, it's possible," Freddie said.

"Was that so hard?" I said.

"Degree of difficulty is not the cause of my resistance," he said, laughing.

"How big was the lump?" I said, finally getting a bit of traction.

"About the size of a golf ball," he said.

"Was there any bleeding?"

"No, just a lot of scotch and water," he deadpanned. "Administered separately."

Josie snorted. I chose to ignore her.

"Where was the lump?"

"It was on the right side of the lower occiput," he said, taking his feet off the desk and sitting up in his chair. "Occiput is the term for the back of the skull in case you were wondering."

"Thanks for clarifying that," I said, making a face at him. I reached behind my head and felt around. "Where exactly was the lump?"

"Let me show you," he said as he got up from his chair and stood behind me. "It's was right there." Then he flicked his finger against the back of my head.

"Ow, that hurt," I said.

"Good."

"You're so going to pay for that," I said, rubbing the spot.

"Oh, I have no doubt about that," Freddie said. "But it was totally worth it. Now, if you ladies will excuse me, I have a lunch meeting to get to."

"Thanks for your help, Freddie," Josie said, getting up out of her chair.

"It was the least I could do," Freddie deadpanned.

"Yes, I noticed," I said, continuing to rub the back of my head.

Chapter 21

Saturday morning was cool, but the wind had finally dropped to a gentle breeze. At nine, a crew arrived to erect a large tent on the lawn. They also installed about a dozen portable heaters that ringed the structure. In the afternoon, Chef Claire and three assistants started organizing plates, napkins, and cutlery, along with several warming trays on long tables that stretched across one side of the tent.

As soon as we were satisfied that our guests would be warm and well-fed, Josie and I headed inside to get ready for the party. Since we also had plans to duck out later that evening, we took the time to put black track suits and running shoes in the car to wear when we went to the boat.

For the party, we both decided to go with jeans and a sweater. The invitation had stressed casual, a consideration we knew all our friends would appreciate. At this time of year, fashion took a back seat to comfort and warmth.

At five, the first guests started arriving and after saying hello most of them headed straight for the buffet table where Chef Claire had an impressive collection of appetizers on display. Josie and I sampled each one, went back for seconds on the spinach rolls and the bacon wrapped figs, then spent the next hour greeting people as they arrived. Jackson arrived with his mom and dad at six, soon followed by Freddie who was traveling solo.

"Hey, guys," Freddie said. "You both look great."

"Hi, Freddie," Josie said.

"Suzy, I was wondering if you could take a look at the bump on the back of my head," he said, grinning.

"You'll get yours, Freddie," I said, glaring at him over the top of my wine glass.

"Hey, Chloe," he said, bending down to pet her. "How are you doing, girl?"

Chloe rolled over on her back and kicked her legs as Freddie scratched her belly.

"She gets that from her mother," Josie said.

I glared at her but didn't have time for a comeback because I saw my mother and Dirk Sinclair walking toward us. They were both dressed in what I call elegant casual.

"How much do you think it costs to look like that?" Josie said.

"You mean dress to make it appear like you couldn't care less what you look like?" I said, laughing.

"Yeah," Josie said. "But she does look great."

"Yes, she does," I said. "And very happy."

"Are you having second thoughts about what we're doing?"

"No. My mom needs to know, and it's better for her to find out now instead of later," I said.

"Yeah, I guess you're right."

"What on earth are you talking about?" Freddie said.

"I'm just babbling," I said. "It must be the concussion you gave me."

"Funny," Freddie said.

"Darling, what a wonderful party," my mother said, gushing and kissing me on the cheek.

"Hi, Mom. How are you doing, Dirk?"

"Hi, Suzy," he said, nodding like a bobble head doll. "I'm good. I'm *really, really* good. Hi, Josie."

"Hey, *Dirk*," Josie said. "Hi, Mrs. C."

"How are you, dear?" my mother said as she hugged Josie. "Hi, Freddie. Tragic news about that boat captain, huh?"

"Yeah, it was. Hi, Dirk," he said, shaking hands.

"How's that Beemer I sold you running?" Dirk said to Freddie while staring at Josie.

"It's great," Freddie said. "I'm about to put it in the garage until spring. I need a four-wheel drive in the winter."

"Sure, sure," Dirk said, already bored.

Then he must have remembered running into Freddie the other day when he was with another woman because his expression changed dramatically. He frowned, stared off into the distance, then forced a smile and looked at Freddie.

"Well, just let me know if you need anything. I'll personally make sure you get a great deal." He turned to my mother. "Should we go sample what my newest chef has come up with today?"

"That sounds wonderful, Dirkie," my mother said, reaching out to take his hand.

"Oh, there you are!"

All of us turned to look at the blonde woman who was strolling across the lawn in our direction. Freddie's description had been accurate. She was young and pretty, blond and extremely well-endowed. I glanced away to look at Dirk and nudged Josie with my arm.

"He's in shock," I said, trying to hide my grin.

"Electroshock, maybe," Josie whispered.

Dirk took a step back but was trapped, and he knew it. He forced a smile in the woman's direction, then glanced at my mother who continued staring at the unfamiliar person walking directly toward her boyfriend. Dirk attempted a casual hug, but the woman pulled him tight and planted a kiss on him that made me blush. The kiss caused a slightly different reaction from my mother.

"Dirk, who is this woman?" my mother said, staring in disbelief at what she was seeing.

"Oh, I've missed you so much," the woman said, rubbing herself against Dirk. "Our little afternoon session the other day wasn't nearly enough."

"What are you doing here, Cindy?" Dirk finally managed to stammer.

"Silly, I was invited," the young blonde named Cindy said. "Didn't this come from you?"

She reached into her purse and pulled out the invitation that Josie and I had slid into her mailbox. It hadn't been easy, but we'd managed to track her down through the restaurant where she and Dirk had eaten lunch.

"Uh, actually," Dirk said, glancing back and forth between her and my mother. "No, it wasn't me. But it's good to see you."

"That's odd," Cindy said, tucking the invitation back in her purse. "But it doesn't matter. I'm here now." She snuggled tight against his chest.

"Dirk?" my mother said quietly.

I recognized the voice immediately. I'd heard that tone hundreds of times in my life. Even when it wasn't directed at me, it still made the hairs on the back of my neck stand up.

"I can explain," Dirk said, frantically looking around for what I assumed was an escape route.

"I can't wait to hear this," Josie whispered.

"He better hurry," I whispered back. "She's about to blow."

"I'm waiting for an explanation, Dirk," my mother said.

"Relax, Grandma," Cindy snapped, slowly turning her head to glare at my mother.

"Uh-oh," Josie whispered. "She played the age card. Big mistake."

135

"They don't come any bigger," I whispered.

I watched my mother's face go stone cold, and I knew that whatever plans she'd had for her and Dirk had just vanished into the cool night air.

"Don't you have someplace to be, dear?" my mother said. "Like maybe cheerleading practice."

"Sure, Grandma," Cindy said, not backing down. "Dirk likes it when I play the schoolgirl role, don't you, sweetie?"

I was sure Dirk loved it, but he wasn't talking.

"I've even got the uniform," Cindy continued. "I'd lend it you, but given your advanced years, I doubt if you could pull it off."

My mother leaped forward and went for the young woman's throat. Dirk managed to get between them and Josie and I pulled my mother back. She was breathing deeply, and her eyes went dark. She continued to glare at Dirk.

"I think I should probably leave," Dirk said, glancing around at all of us.

"Already? But I just got here," Cindy said.

"Let's go," Dirk whispered. Then he looked at my mother. "I'm sorry."

"Yes, a sorry excuse for a man," my mother said.

"Well, I guess I'll see you around," he said, nodding his head at Cindy.

"For your sake, Dirk, let's hope not," my mother said.

He turned and walked away pulling Cindy by the elbow. Freddie excused himself and headed for the bar.

"Are you okay, Mom?"

"No, darling. I'm not."

"But you will be, right?" I said.

"I'm surprised you even have to ask that question."

Way to go, Mom. She's tough as nails when the chips are down.

"I should have seen this coming," she said.

"How could you have known?" Josie said.

"From years of experience," she said.

"You deserve much better, Mom."

"Yes, I do, darling," she said, nodding. "What do you say we grab a drink and see what Chef Claire has whipped up?"

"I could eat," Josie said.

We slowly started walking across the lawn toward the tent that was now full of guests. My mother reached down and took my hand.

"Suzy?"

"Yes, Mom."

"You set that whole thing up, didn't you?"

"Yes, Mom."

"Thank you, darling."

Chapter 22

We drove into town and parked on a small side street near the docks. Our cover story involved finding and treating a lost dog heard whimpering in the nearby park. It wasn't a perfect alibi by any means, but probably good enough since people had barely looked up from their plates when we told them we needed to duck out for a while. We'd changed into what Josie was now calling our B&E ensembles and headed for the dock where the yacht was moored.

"It looks like the whole town is empty," I said, already feeling the effects of our brisk pace.

"That's probably because everyone is at our place," Josie said.

"Yeah. It's a good party," I said.

"Don't remind me," Josie said. "Right now they're all chowing down on grilled salmon."

"I'm sure Chef Claire will save you some," I said.

"How is she going to do that without losing a finger? You saw how that mob attacked the Beef Wellington," Josie said. "I barely got there in time for seconds."

I laughed and pulled my wool cap further down. It had turned cold again, and the wind was kicking up.

"It would be a good night for criminals to be out doing their thing," I said.

"You mean like breaking into a five million dollar yacht?"

"Forget I even brought it up," I said.

We reached the end of the dock, looked left and right, and seeing no one in sight, made our way down the dock and up the stairway. Soon, we were standing on the deck feeling the boat gently rocking.

"Okay, Columbo," Josie said. "What's the plan?"

"I thought we'd just try to jimmy one of the windows along the side open," I said. "Maybe we'll get lucky and find one that's not locked."

"And here I was worried that you didn't have a plan," Josie said, shaking her head.

"You got a better idea?"

"Every idea I have is better than this," Josie said. "For example, like my idea of heading back to the party."

"Relax," I said. "This won't take long."

I started to work my way along the windows that looked down into the living area below deck. I ran my fingers across the edge of each of the six windows and found them all locked tight. We walked around to the other side and repeated the process with the same result. I put my hands on my hips and looked around.

"I guess we can use one of the gaff hooks to break one of them," I said.

"Sure," Josie said. "Why stop now, right?"

"You said you were going to be supportive," I snapped.

"I'm doing my best, Suzy."

"Well, do better."

We both stopped when we heard footsteps on the dock below. We dropped to our knees and inched our way forward and peered down over the boat at the two people beginning their ascent up the stairway.

"Man, we can't catch a break," I said. "Now what?"

"Suzy, I am not going back in that water," Josie said.

"It's Axel and Claire," I said. "Now that I think about it, I didn't see them at the party."

"Well, think of something," Josie said. "We're sitting ducks out here."

And then I remembered the workman who was installing a new latch on the storage area near the bow.

"I've got an idea," I said. "Follow me."

We crawled on all fours until we were able to hide behind the storage area that sat in front of the wheelhouse.

"I don't think this is going to solve our problem," Josie whispered.

"Shhh. Just give me a minute," I said, trying to find the latch in the darkness.

"Are you sure you left it on the boat?" we heard Axel say.

"Yes, remember when we were cleaning the cushions near the front of the bow the other day?" Claire said. "I got warm and took my sweater off."

Their footsteps were getting closer, and I frantically continued to search for the latch. A flashlight beam flashed near our heads.

"Let's have a look," Axel said. "We're already late for the party."

"And whose fault is that?" Claire said, laughing.

I found the latch and pulled it toward me. The door opened, and Josie and I scrambled inside and pulled the door shut. Although muffled, we could still hear the couple's conversation and the sound of cushions and deck chairs scraping on the deck as they moved.

"It has to be here," Claire said.

"What is it about that sweater?" Axel said.

"My mom gave it to me," she said. "I'd never forgive myself if I lost it."

"What a sweet kid," I whispered.

The inside of the storage area was cramped, and we were hunched over with our knees and elbows touching.

"I'm missing out on crab-stuffed lobster tails for this?" Josie whispered.

"Shhh."

"I need to change positions," Josie whispered. "My legs are starting to cramp."

"Just don't make any noise."

I felt Josie pretzel her way into a sitting position. I had no idea how she'd managed it, and I certainly wasn't going to try mimicking her moves. So I stayed put on my hands and knees. In the darkness, I heard the unmistakable sound of a candy bar being unwrapped.

"Really?"

"Hiding in storage areas always makes me hungry," Josie whispered. "You want a bite?"

"What is it?"

"A Snickers."

"No, thanks. I'm good," I said.

We heard a jubilant woman whoop outside on the deck.

"Great," Axel said. "Let's get out of here. I hope there's still some food left when we get there."

"You and me both, pal," Josie whispered through a mouthful of chocolate.

We heard the muffled sound of footsteps on the deck and a few minutes later the sound of them chatting as they headed down the dock.

"Okay, they're gone," Josie said. "Let's get out of here. It's claustrophobic in here. And I can't see my hand in front of my face."

"I noticed you didn't have any trouble finding that candy bar," I said, laughing and reaching for the latch.

"C'mon, let's go," Josie said.

"Uh-oh," I said.

"Suzy?"

"What?"

141

"Define what you mean by uh-oh."

"It's stuck."

"What?"

"Or maybe it locks from the outside," I said.

"Well, isn't that just perfect," Josie said.

"Relax? Just give me a minute," I said, sliding a hand across the walls of the confined space.

"Wait," Josie said. "There's something against my foot."

"What is it?"

"It feels like a handle. Should I try pulling it?"

"I guess it couldn't hurt," I said.

But as Josie felt compelled to remind me on a regular basis for the next several months, I was wrong.

I heard a loud click and then the floor of the storage area we were sitting on disappeared. We dropped through the darkness, and one of us screamed. I think it was me. Seconds later, we landed hard on a soft mattress sprawled across each other in the dark.

"We really need to stop meeting like this," Josie said.

Then we both started giggling uncontrollably.

I rolled over and found a light on a night table next to the bed. We looked around at the elegant master stateroom. Then we stared up at the hole and the drop down ceiling equipped with a small set of stairs.

"Why on earth would anybody design something like that?" Josie said.

I reached up and pulled the bottom step, and the stairs unfolded perfectly and reached the floor.

"It's probably an emergency exit of some sort," I said. "If there was ever a fire in the galley, you might not be able to get out through the door on the other side."

"I guess that makes sense," Josie said, staring up at the hole in the ceiling.

"I don't think the guy who swapped out the latches knew what he was doing," I said. "But at least the release latch worked. Can you imagine getting stuck in that storage area?"

And then a lightbulb went off.

"What is it?" Josie said, noticing the change in my expression.

"I'm not sure yet," I said. "C'mon, let's have a look around."

"Why not? That is why we're here, right?"

We left the stateroom and entered the living quarters that contained a comfortable sitting area and the galley. The head and shower were located on one side along with a couple of additional storage areas. The renovation looked complete, but some pieces of the composite material used to replace the granite and wood were stacked near the main door that led to the upper deck.

"This stuff looks awful," Josie said. "The guy who's buying this boat must be a real nut job."

"Yeah, I agree. I thought the wood and granite were perfect."

"But it is light," Josie said, hefting one of the pieces.

Another lightbulb went off, and my stomach dropped.

"C'mon, let's take a look in the engine room," I said, heading for another door that I assumed would take us down to the bottom of the boat.

We walked down the small set of stairs and glanced around at the area where the engine and most of the boat's machinery were housed. It was spotless.

"That's odd," I said, pointing down at the floor.

"What?" Josie said. "All I see are some bolts sticking up."

"Exactly," I said. "Why would a new boat need something like that?"

"Maybe they plan on adding something in later like another engine. Or maybe air conditioning?"

"Really? Air conditioning?"

"Hey, I'm just spitballing here," Josie snapped. "We've already figured out that the owner is probably a little goofy. Who knows what he's thinking about adding later?"

"No, I don't think the bolts are there for something that's going to be added in later. I think the bolts are all that's left of something that's already been removed."

"Like what?" Josie said.

"I don't know," I said. "But whatever it was, I'm willing to bet that it was very heavy."

"Should I ask why?"

"Not yet," I said, heading up the stairs. "I'm still thinking."

"I thought I smelled something burning," Josie said, laughing.

Back in the galley area, I started going through the cabinets. In one of the larger ones next to the head, I found a thin cylindrical object about four feet long. I turned it over in my hands and frowned.

"What's that thing?" Josie said.

"I have no idea," I said, examining the label. "Have you got your phone with you?"

"Sure."

"Can you get a wireless signal?"

Josie checked and then nodded.

"There's the name of the manufacturer and an item number on the label. Google it and see what you get."

Josie leaned over my shoulder and typed the information into the search bar. Seconds later, she looked at me.

"It's a portable draft measurement device," Josie said. "Does that make any sense to you?"

"Sadly, yes."

"What's going on, Suzy?"

"C'mon, let's put everything back the way it was and get back to the party."

"Are you okay?"

"No, I'm not even close to okay."

Chapter 23

The party was still going strong when we got home. As we strolled across the lawn, I scanned the crowd. Chef Claire was sitting at a table with her catering crew, relaxing and enjoying a glass of wine. We stopped next to the table to say hello.

"How's everything going?" I said, glancing around the party.

"It's great," Chef Claire said. "They all seemed to love the food. And the crab stuffed lobster tails just disappeared."

Josie moaned softly, and Chef Claire laughed.

"Don't worry," Chef Claire said to Josie. "I saved you a couple."

"You're so good," Josie said.

"Suzy, I heard about what he did to your mom," Chef Claire said. "That's inexcusable."

"Yes, it is," I said.

"As soon as I heard the news, I called Dirk and turned the job down."

"You did?" Josie said.

She couldn't contain her excitement, and she grabbed my forearm and squeezed it hard.

"Really?" I said, freeing myself from Josie's death grip. "So what do you think you'll do now?"

"I'll probably just head south anyway," Chef Claire said. "I hear that some good things are happening in the food scene in the Carolinas. I'm sure I'll find something. And if worse comes to worse, maybe I'll just reopen my food truck and start driving across the country until I land in the right spot."

"What a great idea," one of Chef Claire's crew said.

"Yeah, that's fantastic," another crew member said. "You know, that would make a great reality TV show."

I scowled at both of them. Chef Claire seemed to be giving the idea serious consideration.

"Actually, it's not a bad idea," Chef Claire said.

"Nothing ever sounds like a bad idea this late at night," I said, glancing at Josie.

"Yes, let's not spoil the evening with a bunch of crazy schemes," Josie said. "We can talk about all that later."

"I think I'll hit the dessert table," I said.

"Good idea," Josie said, following me. "We need to come up with a plan soon."

"I know. But it's going to have to wait for now," I said, spying Jackson sitting at a table next to Alice.

"You heard her," Josie said. "She's already moved on to Plan B." Then she stared at the blank expression on my face. "What on earth is wrong with you?"

"Hang on," I said. "I'll be back in a few minutes."

Despite my despondent mood, I snuck a quick peek at the dessert table, and the supply seemed to be holding steady. But just to be sure, I grabbed a couple of cannoli as I walked past the table on my way toward Jackson and Alice. Josie hovered around the desserts before sitting back down next to Chef Claire.

"There you are. How did it go?" Jackson said, glancing up as I approached.

"Oh, it was fine," I said, sitting down. "Hey, Alice."

"Hi, Suzy," Alice said.

"I hear you guys are finally all set to take off," I said.

"Finally. The first thing Monday morning. I can't wait," she said. "Did something happen tonight?"

"Oh, Josie and I just needed to check something out," I said, forcing myself to maintain eye contact.

"A dog?" she said.

"Absolutely," I said, taking a bite of cannoli.

"The poor thing. Is it going to be okay?" Alice said.

"I think it's too soon to tell, but I'm keeping my fingers crossed. You aren't overdoing it are you, Jackson?"

"No, I'm good," he said, stretching in his chair. "Apart from being stuffed to the gills, that is."

"Tell me about it," Alice said. "I can't believe how much I ate."

"Jackson, I need to grab something from the house. Would you mind giving me a hand?"

"Sure," he said, standing up. "Excuse me for a few minutes, Alice. I hope we can finish talking about this later."

"That would be great," she said. "I need to tell you a few more things."

Alice got up and headed toward the table where my mother and John were chatting. My mother caught my eye and waved. She even managed a smile, but I knew she was still struggling with what had happened earlier. When Alice reached the table, John gestured to the seat next to him and Alice sat down. He patted her leg, let his hand rest on her thigh for a moment, and then removed it.

Josie fell in step next to us as we headed for the house.

"Are you finally ready to tell me what's rolling around inside your head?" Josie said, holding the door open.

"I'm going to try," I said, heading for the living room.

We said hello to Chloe and sat down. I waved off Josie's offer of wine but did take a few seconds to polish off my second cannoli.

"So what did you need help with?" Jackson said.

"Nothing," I said. "It was a ruse to get you up here so we could talk in private."

"A ruse? What's going on?" Jackson said, glancing back and forth between Josie and me.

"I have no idea," Josie said. "She's been acting weird ever since we left the boat."

Josie realized her mistake and sighed loudly.

"Sorry," she said.

"What on earth are you two talking about?" Jackson said. "What boat?"

"John's boat," I said eventually. "The yacht down at the dock."

"Why were you snooping around John's boat?" Jackson said.

"Who says we were snooping?" I said.

Josie snorted. My comment even sounded lame to me.

"Okay, so we were snooping," I said.

"I'm still waiting for an explanation," Jackson said, giving me a hard stare.

"The boat is the key to the murders," I said.

"Murders?" Jackson said. "As in plural?"

"Yes, Roger the Engineer and Captain Bill."

Jackson blinked, then rubbed his eyes. I knew what was coming and waited it out.

"Suzy, I can't begin to tell you how much I appreciate everything you and Josie have done for me. Not to mention what a great job you did with Sluggo. But you are way out of your league on this one. You need to leave the murder investigation to the people who do these things for a living. And nobody thinks Captain Bill was murdered. He was just a drunk who happened to fall into the water and drown."

"Everybody is wrong," I said.

"And, of course, you can prove this," Jackson said.

"Not yet," I said, shaking my head.

"Well, there you go," he said. "You know, I always hate it when things are missing. It really gets in the way of solving crimes."

"What things?" I said.

"The mysterious and elusive things us cops like to call facts."

"The facts are all there," I said. "They just need to be *revealed.*"

"Is that all?" Jackson said. "I feel so much better."

Josie laughed.

"Yes," I said. "Revealed then confirmed."

"Let's not get ahead of ourselves," Jackson said, leaning back in his chair and giving me a less than inviting smile. "Why don't we start by you telling me what you think you've figured out?"

"That would be great," Josie said. "Because I don't have a clue where you're going with this, Suzy."

I started talking and kept talking for the next twenty minutes. By the time I finished, Jackson was sitting in stunned silence and staring at me like I was from another planet.

Even Josie was staring at me like I'd lost my mind.

Chapter 24

The sun was just starting to appear over the horizon on Monday morning when Josie, Jackson, and I strolled down the dock as if we didn't have a care in the world. It was cold and breezy. A foggy mist hovered just above the surface of the water, and I heard squawking and the flutter of wings as the waterfowl woke and got ready for the day.

I shifted the picnic basket I was carrying to my other hand and then set it down on the dock when we reached the stairway that led up to the boat. Jackson was carrying a case of champagne, and Josie held a large bouquet of fresh cut flowers in one hand and a box of Paterson's doughnuts in the other. So far, my strategy to give her the bouquet to occupy her free hand had worked perfectly, and all the doughnuts survived the trip to the boat.

Up on deck, the crew was making final preparations for departure and John stood mid-deck nodding and chatting with Alice. When he saw us standing on the dock, he waved and motioned for us to come aboard. We handed all the items we'd brought up the stairway in an assembly line fashion, then climbed aboard.

"What a nice surprise," John said. "What are you guys doing here?"

"We just thought we'd give you a proper sendoff," I said, waving at Alice as well as Axel and Sheila who were wiping dew from the furniture and railings.

"How nice," John said. "Let's head below deck. It's cold up here, and we've got a pot of fresh coffee. And I think I see a box of doughnuts from Paterson's." He laughed. "It'll be a while before I get a chance to eat them again. I'm sure I'll go into withdrawal by the time we hit the Erie Canal."

He and Alice led us down the stairs into the sitting area next to the galley. John looked more relaxed than he had in weeks. I assumed now that the boat was ready to go, he could kick back and enjoy the long trip to Florida. John poured coffee, and Josie passed the box of doughnuts around after grabbing two. After the box had made its way around the table, it ended up sitting right in front of her.

I noticed the loving look she was giving the four remaining doughnuts.

"You need to focus," I whispered to her.

"Oh, don't worry," she whispered, still staring down at the box. "I'm very focused."

"Josie," I whispered as I dug my fingernails into her thigh under the table. "You need to pay attention."

"Ow," she whispered, squirming out of my grip. "Don't worry. I'll be listening closely to you crash and burn. I plan on retelling this story many times in the future, and I want to make sure I get it right. And for the record, I can listen and eat at the same time."

"Thanks for all your support," I whispered through clenched teeth.

We'd been going back and forth about how I should handle the situation. In the end, I'd decided to go for strong and direct. Josie was still advocating for heavy sedation and a long stay in a room with padded walls.

"Are you two okay?" John said, watching our sidebar.

"Yeah, we're fine," I said. "But it's probably a good idea for you to keep a close eye on your doughnut."

John laughed, and Josie made a face at me and took a sip of coffee.

"You didn't need to do this," John said, patting the top of the case of champagne. "But I'm sure we'll put it to good use. And those flowers are beautiful. I'll find a vase for them later."

"And Chef Claire stuffed the picnic basket full of goodies," I said.

"You guys are the best," John said.

"Yeah, we have our moments," I said, glancing at Jackson, who was looking down at his phone. When he looked up and caught my eye, he nodded for me to proceed.

As we had discussed on the way over, if my theory didn't get traction immediately, I would drop the whole thing. I had spent hours formulating my first question. Now was the time to put it out there. And on the threshold of initiating a conversation that might forever change my friendship with someone who'd been an important part of my life for years, for a moment I wished I'd never allowed my thoughts to drift in the direction they'd gone.

"The boat looks great, John," I said. Then I took a deep breath and tossed the question out in the same quick and efficient manner I used to cast my line into the shallows. "So tell me, how much weight did you have to remove to pull the draft back to five feet?"

Alice flinched but immediately recovered. But what I, along with Jackson and Josie, was interested in was John's reaction. His eyes grew wide, then narrowed as he frowned briefly, then a grin emerged. It had only taken a few seconds, but all three of us saw it.

"What on earth are you talking about, Suzy?" John said.

"The draft of the boat. The day it arrived, we were talking about the requirements for traveling the Inland Waterway and you mentioned that a boat couldn't have a draft any deeper than five feet."

"What about it?" he said, frowning as he glanced around the room.

"Well, ever since the boat arrived, it seems that all you've been doing, under the guise of renovation, is try to make the boat lighter," I said.

"Under the *guise* of renovation?" John said, glaring at me. "Would you mind telling me the point you're trying to make?"

"It just seems like you've spent an awful lot of time on it," I said. "I think it's odd. Some people might even call it suspicious."

His gave me a hard stare. I almost wilted, but hung tough.

"Who do you think you're talking to, Suzy?"

"I don't know who I'm talking to, John," I said. "I thought I did. Now, I'm not so sure."

"Look, we've got a very long trip ahead of us, and I'd really like to get going. So why don't you tell me exactly what you're trying to say?"

"I'm saying that this boat is the key to the murder of both your engineer and Captain Bill."

There it was. I'd somehow found the courage to put it out there on the table for everyone to see, right next to the last four doughnuts.

Then I glanced at Josie who was slowly chewing. She looked at me and shrugged.

"What?" she said.

I had no idea when she'd taken it, but we were down to three doughnuts. I shook my head and looked at John who continued giving me a dark stare.

"How is the boat connected to Roger's death, Suzy?" John said, folding his arms across his chest.

"I was hoping you'd be willing to tell us, John," I said. "Given your involvement, why don't you enlighten us?"

Jackson stared at me, and I'm sure he thought I'd gone way too far, way too fast with the conversation.

"My involvement? Suzy, we go way back, and I treasure our friendship, but you've crossed the line here," John said, "Jackson, I'd like you to remove this woman from my boat. As of this moment, I consider her to be trespassing."

"In a minute, John," Jackson said, returning John's stare.

"This is unbelievable," John said, shaking his head.

"Should I continue?" I said.

"Of course," John said, laughing. "I can't wait to hear where this conversation is going to go next."

"The day the boat arrived, Alice mentioned that Captain Bill and Roger had been arguing non-stop since they'd left Montreal."

"So what?" John said, glancing at Alice. "They argued about everything."

"Perhaps," I said. "But I think this time they were arguing about who was responsible for the screw-up."

"Screw up?" John said, his eyes widening again.

"Yes, the math problem," I said. "We were talking that afternoon, and you mentioned how those two *geniuses*, Captain Bill and Roger, had difficulties understanding basic math."

"I don't remember saying that at all," John said.

"I do," Josie said.

That's my girl. In the end, Josie always has my back. I leaned over to whisper a thank you then glanced down and noticed we were down to two doughnuts. The way they were disappearing right before my eyes, I wondered if she'd been taking magic lessons.

John glared at Josie and then refocused on me. I took a moment to gather my thoughts then continued.

"And when you told us that the owner wanted to swap out that beautiful granite and wood interior for that crappy composite, it didn't make any sense. Nobody would do that, no matter how eccentric they were. But it is very light, isn't it?"

"So?" John said, spreading his hands.

"But that still didn't give you enough of the draft back. When we were here last week, the supervisor of the renovation crew was talking about how he needed to find four more. You said he was talking about needing four more workers. But he was really talking about finding four more inches of draft, wasn't he?"

"You need to leave now, Suzy. Go back to your dogs where you belong."

"And since the interior renovation didn't give you enough, you had to start removing some things from the engine room, right?"

He stared at me in disbelief.

"How would you know anything about my engine room?" John said. "Jackson, this woman has obviously been on this boat without permission. I want you to arrest her, both of them, for trespassing, breaking and entering and anything else I can think of."

"Don't worry, John," Jackson said. "I'm definitely considering it. But let's keep talking for a minute."

"Okay. But as soon as we finish up with this nonsense, you're done in this town," John said. "Trust me. I'm going to make it one of my personal missions."

"I can live with that, John," Jackson said. "I've always wanted to go into the grocery business."

"Anybody who sees those bolts sticking up out of the floor in the engine room will come to the same conclusion," I said. "A couple of heavy pieces of equipment were recently removed."

"Suzy, I think you've lost your mind," John said, then turned to Jackson. "Are you listening to her? This woman is insane."

"She does have her moments. I have to give you that," Jackson said.

I glared at him, then caught the smile on his face.

"I was doing a bit of math on my own," I said.

"Good for you," John said, shaking his head again.

"This boat is about sixty-five feet long with a beam around nineteen feet. A yacht this size usually weighs in at around a hundred thousand pounds fully loaded, give or take a few thousand. Does that sound about right?"

John shrugged and continued to stare at me.

"I used an online tool I found that calculates a boat's draft based on length, width, and total weight."

"And?" John said, raising an eyebrow.

"And by my calculations, about every fifteen hundred pounds of weight adds an inch of draft. So you needed to remove several thousand pounds to reduce about half a foot of draft so you could make the Inland Waterway trip."

John stood up and leaned with his back against the galley counter.

"So if Captain Bill and Roger made a wrong calculation, and I'm not saying they did, what's the big deal?"

"The big deal is how the mistake got made in the first place and why it's important."

"I can't wait to hear this," John said, laughing.

"You know, John," I said, "I couldn't understand what math problem they could have made. Roger had been building boats for you for years. And Captain Bill was obviously very experienced. At least when he was sober. Then I remembered that Captain Bill was an American, but Roger was Canadian."

"And you think that's what caused this math problem?" John said, continuing to laugh.

"Yes. The metric system," I said.

John's face dropped, then he recovered. He took a sip of coffee and pushed the plate holding his doughnut to one side. That was the moment I knew I had him. Nobody with a clear conscious would ever do that to a Paterson's doughnut.

"What does the metric system have to do with the price of fish?" John said.

"By itself, nothing. But when I remembered the one place where the metric system is frequently used in the States, it became clear," I said, choking back my emotions. "And I have to tell you, John, when I finally put it all together, it broke my heart."

John glanced at Alice whose face was drained of color.

"The math problem occurred when Captain Bill and Roger somehow got pounds and kilograms mixed up. Since a kilogram is a little over two pounds, five to ten thousand kilograms misread as pounds adds up to a lot of weight. And about a half a foot of draft that needed to be eliminated."

"What exactly are you trying to accuse me of, Suzy?" John said.

"Smuggling," I whispered.

"Smuggling what?"

"Given Captain Bill's history working in places like Afghanistan and Turkey, my guess is heroin."

Alice gasped, and she gave John a wide-eyed look.

"Relax, Alice," John said. "Suzy, even if I were inclined toward criminal behavior of that sort, do you think I'd be stupid enough to put several thousand pounds of drugs on this boat?"

"No, John," I said. "I don't. I think you put it *in* the boat."

John's head snapped back like I'd slapped him, but again he recovered. Then he forced another laugh.

Apparently, he was determined to go down swinging.

"My guess is that there are somewhere between five and ten thousand kilos inside the hull of this boat. That would be pretty easy to do since you and Roger built it. The heroin probably got unloaded off a ship in Montreal, and now it's tucked safe and sound along both sides of this boat. I also guess that the story about the owner in Florida is a total lie. This boat is all yours. You aren't selling it to anybody."

John stared at me, then nodded. He glanced at Alice and reached behind him. Jackson stood up and pointed his gun at John.

"Easy does it, John," Jackson said. "I really don't want to shoot you."

John slowly revealed his hand. It was holding his doughnut.

"No need for that, Jackson," John said, laughing. "If you want a bite, all you have to do is ask."

He took a bite and smiled at Jackson. Jackson slowly lowered the gun until it pointed down at the floor. Jackson froze when he felt the touch of cold metal against his temple.

"Easy does it, Jackson," Alice said, her hand trembling as she held the gun to his head.

"Good girl," John said as he stepped forward to take Jackson's gun. He pointed it at us and moved back to his previous spot. Alice pointed her gun at us and stood slightly behind John a safe distance away from three of us who remained sitting at the table.

"Suzy, you are simply too much," John said. "I have to say that I'm very impressed with how you put that together. And if you had ever gotten tired of working with dogs, I'm sure the FBI would have gladly found a spot for you."

"He's already speaking in the past tense," Josie whispered. "That can't be good."

"No," I whispered. "It's not."

I glanced down at the last remaining doughnut in the box.

"Really?"

"What?" Josie whispered. "You want the last one?"

"You're unbelievable," I said.

"Relax. He's not going to shoot us here," Josie said.

159

"We'll be heading out soon so just kick back and try to enjoy yourself. Eat all the doughnuts you want," John said. "But Josie's right. Shooting you here at the dock isn't an option."

"I told you," Josie whispered.

"But later on tonight, you'll get a chance to experience just how cold Lake Ontario is this time of year," John said.

"Do you remember that day when you mentioned going waterskiing one last time for the season?" I said.

"Sure," John said, nodding.

"You didn't go waterskiing, did you?"

"No, actually I was in the water right below where you're sitting," he said. "I needed to make sure the draft measurement instrument I was using was accurate. As I'm sure you can understand, I have a lot at stake financially and just can't run the risk of running aground on the Waterway."

"It's a good plan, John," I said.

"Yes, I know," he said. "It's brilliant."

"Most people carrying that much heroin would be doing everything they could to stay out of sight. But your plan is to be out on the water in plain sight hoping everyone sees you and this beautiful boat. You'll probably even give tours to people who want to take a look."

"Sure," he said, laughing. "I've got nothing to hide."

"John, I have a question," Jackson said.

"Sure, Jackson. Shoot." Then he cackled and glanced back at Alice. "Oh, that's right you can't because I have your gun."

"Funny," Jackson said. "My question is why? You don't need this sort of trouble."

"Actually, Jackson," John said. "The truth is I do. I've made some business decisions over the past several years that could be considered *questionable*. But this one deal will put an end to my money worries forever."

"And what about you, Alice?" I said.

"What about me?" she said, pointing the gun in my direction.

"Are you doing this because of him?" I said, nodding at John.

For some reason, they both found my question particularly funny.

"No, Suzy," Alice said. "John and I have an understanding, and I'm sure that situation will continue throughout our trip, but then I'm sure we'll both go our separate ways."

"Absolutely," John said. "And I have to admire your integrity and restraint, Jackson. This girl is amazing. You don't know what you're missing."

Josie and I looked at Jackson.

"You didn't sleep with her?" Josie said.

"Of course I didn't sleep with her," Jackson snapped. "She was my summer intern."

"I certainly gave it my best shot," Alice said. "But he's so resolute. Jackson is a cop's cop. It was shortly after that I decided a career in criminology wasn't for me and I started to consider John's offer."

"But why?" I said.

"I told you before, Suzy. I like the lifestyle. A lot." She looked at John. "Can we please get going? I need to get out of this town."

"It won't be long," John said. "But I'd like to hear Suzy's thoughts about the rest of it."

"You mean the murders?" I said.

"I prefer to call it the removal of two staff members who'd outlived their usefulness, but sure, let's go with murder," John said, chuckling.

"Did you hear that, Alice?" I said. "I hope you've got a good contingency plan for when you arrive in Florida."

Alice glanced at John, who waved my comment off.

"She's got nothing to worry about. And unlike those two other idiots, Alice knows how to keep her mouth shut. Go ahead, Suzy. Dazzle me with your detective abilities."

I sat back in my chair and composed my thoughts. Then I launched in.

"Let's start with Captain Bill since he's the easy one. We saw him with Alice at the Water's Edge that afternoon," I said.

"I didn't kill him," Alice said, vigorously shaking her head.

"I know you didn't," I said. "John did. Millie confirmed that you left the Water's Edge sometime before she cut Captain Bill off at five. But before you left, you told him to meet you back at the boat later that night. I think you had a little thing going on with him. But I'm sure you did that as a way to control him rather than any real attraction you had for him."

"You're good," John said.

"I have my moments. And you both knew that Captain Bill would kill time until he was supposed to meet you by drinking some more. By the time he reached the boat, he would have been easy pickings for John, who was probably hiding on the boat or somewhere on the dock. Now that I think about it, it was probably the dock because you wouldn't want to run the risk of getting blood on the boat."

"Continue," John said, nodding.

"You hit him on the back of the head and made sure he got wedged between the boat and the piling. By the time his body was discovered, the bump on his head was logically written off as just one more bruise."

"Fascinating," John said. "Are you sure you don't want to come to work for me, Suzy? You'd make an awful lot of money."

"I have enough money, John," I said. "What I never have enough of are dogs and friends. And I'm down one good friend at the moment."

"Yeah," John said. "I'm truly sorry about that. You're a good woman who means well. Pity you can't stop sticking your nose where it doesn't belong."

"I guess we all have our minor imperfections, right?" I said.

Josie snorted.

"But we were good friends, weren't we?" John said softly.

"Yes, we were."

"Well, I guess stuff happens," he said, shrugging. "But I know you'll put that three hundred grand to good use."

"We were thinking about naming the rescue program after you," Josie said.

"What about now?" John said, laughing.

"Only as a memorial," Josie said.

"I'm going to miss you, Josie," he said, staring at her. "You truly are one of the most beautiful women I've ever met. We could have had a lot of fun together."

"Put the gun down, and we'll see if there's still a chance," Josie said.

"Funny," John said. Then he turned back to me. "So, tell me, Suzy. What are your thoughts about what happened to Roger?"

"I didn't have a clue until the other night," I said. "Now I think I've put the timeline together. You killed Roger at some point during the time Summerman was playing. The way he holds an audience's attention, nobody would have been paying attention to you and Roger heading for the boat."

John slowly nodded his head.

"Go on," he said.

"But you needed two things to happen. First, you needed the body to be found. If Roger just disappeared, that could have caused a serious manhunt with cops and investigators on both sides of the River hanging around for a long time asking a whole bunch of questions. Maybe they would have wanted to do a close inspection of the boat. And it might have delayed your departure for weeks. Who knows? But it was certainly a risk you didn't want to take. So you decided to put the body on display. Second, you needed an alibi."

"Yes, I did," he said, grinning. "And how did I manage to pull that off?"

"That was the tricky part," I said. "And I have to commend you. It was brilliant."

"Yes, it was," he said.

"You killed him during Summerman's show, and then you hid the body. After the show, I remember you made a big deal of taking a bunch of people on a tour of the boat before the check presentation. You showed everyone this area and the stateroom in the back. But there wasn't a body on the bed during the tour, was there?"

"No," John said, grinning.

"And when you escorted everyone back from the boat, you headed straight for the stage and the check presentation. You were in plain sight the entire time."

"Yes, I certainly was."

I wanted to reach out and slap that stupid grin off his face. But since he and Alice were still pointing guns at me, discretion won out.

"During the check presentation, we all heard the scream. And, yes, as you said on the boat that day, it was muffled. But the scream was a mistake, wasn't it?"

John glanced at Alice, whose face was now completely drained of color.

"Yes, it was," John said. "I'm intrigued. How do you know that?"

"I figured it out the other night when Josie and I were crammed into the storage area in front of the wheelhouse."

"Can I ask you why the two of you were in there?" John said.

"Does it matter?" I said.

"No, I guess not," he said, shrugging. "Continue."

"You put Roger's body in the storage area and gave Alice instructions to use the trap door to drop the body onto the bed down below after you finished giving people the tour. By the way, is that an emergency exit?"

"Yes, it is," John said. "But I discovered that it's useful for other things."

"Like hiding a dead body?"

"Exactly."

"So my guess is that you gave Alice instructions to slip away during the check presentation and head to the storage area and release the latch. The ceiling drops away, Roger's body falls harmlessly onto the bed below, and Alice heads back to the party. It shouldn't have taken more than a couple of minutes."

"Five minutes max," John said.

I glanced at Alice. I assumed she realized she was about to take a trip down bad memory lane.

"But neither of the latches worked very well. I think Alice crawled into the storage area, closed the door behind her, but then couldn't get the latch that released the floor to work. Then she couldn't get the door to the storage area back open, and she was trapped in that very tight space with a dead body."

Tears started streaming down Alice's cheeks.

"I remember your reaction to the two dead bodies you saw during the summer when you were Jackson's intern. You couldn't handle it, could you?"

"No," Alice whispered.

"And when you found yourself trapped in that space with Roger's body, you freaked out and screamed, didn't you?"

"Yes, I was terrified," she said.

"It's okay, Alice. It all worked out in the end," John said. "Try to relax. We'll be out of here soon, and these three certainly won't be telling anybody."

"I wish he'd quit reminding us," Josie whispered.

I patted her hand and continued.

"You finally managed to get the door open, but the floor latch wouldn't work. But since you'd screamed and knew that people had heard it, you knew you had to move fast. You raced below deck into the stateroom. There must be another latch somewhere in there you needed to fiddle with that would make it possible for the ceiling to release. Whatever it was, you figured it out and headed back upstairs. By now, you were completely freaked out, and when you saw Jackson standing there, you panicked and hit him in the back of the head."

"It was dark, and I swear I didn't know it was you, Jackson," Alice said, sobbing uncontrollably. "I could never hurt you. I just saw your silhouette and reacted."

Jackson listened without reacting.

"But you did remember to wipe your prints off the wrench, right?" I said.

"Yes, I did," Alice said. "John has drilled that into my head time and time again."

"You knew that others were undoubtedly on the way, and you raced back to the storage area."

"Yes, I could already see them heading down the dock. I almost stepped on Sluggo on my way out."

"I was wondering about that, Jackson," I said. "Sluggo couldn't have climbed that stairway by himself."

"I carried him up," Jackson said. "I heard him running along the dock and waited a few seconds until he got to me. I didn't have a clue what was happening, and I wasn't about to leave him by himself on the dock. Sluggo is pretty fast when he wants to be."

"You got back into the storage area and, this time, the latch worked, and you dropped the body," I said to Alice. "Then you were able to get it reclosed before anyone made it below deck."

"Barely," Alice whispered. "It was so close."

"The suspense is what makes it such a great story," John said, his eyes wild. "Not that any of us will ever be telling it to anyone." He cackled. "For obvious reasons, of course."

"You stayed in the storage area until everyone had arrived and then you made your way below deck and hung out in the back with the rest of the onlookers. I remember seeing you there. You were just one more party guest wondering what the heck was going on."

Alice nodded and exhaled loudly. She wiped her eyes with the back of her gun hand and looked at John.

"Can we please go now?" she said.

"Sure. I've heard enough. Why don't you head up on deck and see if the snuggle-bunnies are ready to go?" John said, then glanced at the three of us and shook his head. "Those two. They're like rabbits."

Alice started to leave but paused to look back at John.

"What should I do with this?" she said, glancing down at her gun.

"Yeah, you should probably leave that here. There's no reason to scare the rest of the crew yet."

Alice handed the gun to John, and he slid it into his jacket pocket. He sat down across from us at the table and smiled.

"Don't worry, folks," John said. "We'll be getting out of here soon."

"I seriously doubt that," Jackson said.

"What?"

Jackson nodded toward the stairs that led to the top deck. John's mouth dropped when he saw the two guns pointing at his head. Then Jackson nodded toward the stateroom. John slowly turned around and saw Detective Abrams and two of the biggest state policemen I'd ever seen also pointing their guns at him.

"Okay, John," Detective Abrams said. "Let's try not to make any more bad memories. Drop it, then very slowly get your hands way above your head."

John considered his options, then dropped the gun on the floor and slowly raised his hands. Seconds later, he was face down on the floor and handcuffed.

"Did you get all that?" Jackson said.

"Every word," Detective Abrams said. "It was like we were in the room with you."

"I guess the decision to put the device in the flowers was a good one," Jackson said.

"You're welcome," Josie said.

"Well, I'm sure glad we didn't decide to hide it in the doughnuts," I said, shaking my head at the empty box.

"Hey, what can I say?" Josie said. "Getting held at gunpoint always makes me hungry."

Chapter 25

I came to a stop in front of a large two-story brick building that was vacant but located within walking distance of downtown. I turned the SUV off and smiled at Josie who was sitting in the passenger seat.

"I thought we were going to have breakfast at the Café," Chef Claire said from the backseat.

"We are," I said. "We just need to make a quick stop to see my mother."

Chef Claire glanced out the window at the structure that was in need of repair.

"We're meeting your mother here?" Chef Claire said.

"Yes," I said, pointing across the street. "And there she is, right on time. Wonders never cease."

I hopped out of the car and waved to my mother who was crossing the street heading our way.

"Good morning, Mom."

"Hello, darling," she said, bussing my cheek. "Josie, Chef Claire. I hope you ladies are doing well." She looked around at the setting. "It looks like we've hit the peak of our fall foliage. Isn't it beautiful, Chef Claire?"

"Yes, Mrs. C. It is," Chef Claire said, seeming a bit bewildered by my mother's exuberance.

I had to admit that, at first, it caught me off guard as well. But then I remembered that my mother was working, and nothing improved her mood like the prospect of closing a deal.

"Shall we get started?" my mother said, removing a set of keys from her coat pocket.

"Sure, let's do it," I said, following her up the stairs that led to the massive verandah that wrapped around three sides of the building.

"What's going on?" Chef Claire said.

"I just thought you three would be interested in taking a look inside," my mother said, pushing open the front door.

"No offense, Mrs. C., but why would we want to do that?" Chef Claire said.

"Because I just bought it," my mother said.

"Okay," Chef Claire said, shrugging as she stepped inside. She glanced around at the place and shook her head. "It's your money. I guess you can spend it however you please."

"Look at these beautiful hardwood floors," my mother said.

Actually, they were far from beautiful at the moment, but I knew that with some work they would be.

"Oak," my mother said, gently bouncing up and down. "Do you feel that?"

"I don't feel anything," Chef Claire said.

"Exactly," my mother said. "The bones of this place are rock solid. They don't build them like this anymore."

I'd lived in Clay Bay my entire life and had driven by the building thousands of times but had never been inside. I stared up at the rotunda ceiling that was at least thirty feet high at its peak. I tried to calculate the floor space but gave up. I was done with math for a while.

"What's the square footage, Mom?"

"Downstairs is about five thousand," she said. "And the living quarters upstairs is about two."

"Living quarters?" Chef Claire said, laughing. "Don't tell me you're thinking about living here."

"Oh, of course not, my dear," my mother said, chuckling at the thought.

"Then what are you planning to do with it?" Chef Claire said.

"It isn't a question of what I'm going to do with it, Chef Claire. The question is what are you going to do with it?"

"I'm afraid you lost me, Mrs. C."

"This is your place," my mother said.

"What on earth are you talking about?" Chef Claire said, glancing around and seeing the grins on our faces.

"You wanted to open your own place," my mother said, spreading her arms. "Well, here it is."

"Look at that fireplace," Josie said, heading across the room. "This would be the perfect spot for the bar."

"You're right," I said, then looked at Chef Claire. "What do you think?"

"I think you people are out of your minds. I can't afford something like this. The renovations alone would run at least half a million."

"So?" I said.

"So?" Chef Claire said, staring at me. "So that's a lot of money, and in case you haven't noticed, I don't have half a million."

"No," my mother said. "But we do. And as your silent partners, it will be our responsibility to make sure that you have enough working capital to get the restaurant off the ground."

"What? The three of you? Silent partners?" Chef Claire said, leaning against the wall for support.

"Well, silent apart from the clanging of metal you hear every time Josie picks up a knife and fork," I said, laughing.

"You're one to talk," Josie said.

"We need to slow down a bit," Chef Claire said. "How would this work?"

I looked at my mother and nodded for her to start.

"First of all, the three of you will need to set up a corporation," my mother said.

"What about you?" Chef Claire said.

"My dear, trust me, I have absolutely no interest in running a restaurant. As far as your business is concerned, my role will be limited to being your landlord."

"So you're going to rent it to us?"

"Initially, yes," my mother said. "But at some point in the future, I'm sure I'd be willing to consider selling the building to you."

"How much is the rent?" Chef Claire said.

"One dollar a year," my mother said, starting to stroll off into the adjacent room. "This would be a wonderful place to have dinner. How many people do you think this room could hold?"

Chef Claire glanced around and thought about it.

I was glad it was her turn to do the math.

"Probably twenty," she said.

"So if there are four other rooms about this size, the restaurant could seat around a hundred people?" my mother said.

"Yeah, that's probably close," Chef Claire said, glancing around. "If you turned the tables twice a night, you could probably do two hundred dinners on a busy night. Maybe a few more."

"I don't know anything about the restaurant business, but that sounds like enough to make a living," my mother said.

"Sure," Chef Claire said. "But it's a short season."

"Oh, no, my dear," my mother said. "You misunderstood me. There's nothing seasonal about this proposal."

"What?" Chef Claire said.

"We're thinking about a year-round operation," I said. "The town can use a nice place for people to hang out during the winter."

"We'd lose our shirts during the winter," Chef Claire said.

"Not necessarily," Josie said. "Not if we were smart about it."

"We could go to a limited menu with a lot of soups and stews," I said. "We could do pizzas and sandwiches, things like that. Maybe even do in town deliveries. And we'd have the bar business. We'd lose some money, but I'll cover that."

"You'll cover that?" Chef Claire said.

"Sure," I said, shrugging. "I recently came into some money."

Last night my mother and I had agreed that she would advance a portion of my inheritance to fund the restaurant. She'd written me a very large check with a lot of zeroes on the spot. I had stared at the check and blinked several times just to make sure my eyes weren't playing tricks on me. Then my mother had told me not to worry about spending it because it was a very small percentage of my total inheritance. For the first time, I had a pretty good idea of how much money she was worth and, to be honest, it took my breath away.

"Suzy, I can't let you do that," Chef Claire said.

"Why not?" I said.

"Because we could lose thousands of dollars a month during the winter," Chef Claire said.

"Well, if we do, then in about fifty years, we'll probably need to start thinking about shutting the doors," I said.

Josie snorted.

For the first time in weeks, I didn't find it annoying.

"We have a few more stipulations," my mother said.

Chef Claire's face dropped.

"Relax, my dear," my mother said laughing. "You're going to like them."

"Okay, let's hear them," Chef Claire said, again leaning against a wall.

"As the former mayor and current member of the town council, I consider it part of my responsibilities to look for ways to improve the lives of our residents. So, as part of our business arrangement, I'd like to ask you to include some low-cost meals that would be delivered to our shut-ins. Perhaps a daily special of some sort."

"Sure, that's very doable," Chef Claire said, nodding.

"Wonderful," my mother said. "The rest of the Council will be very happy to hear that. And I'm sure that will help us expedite any permits or permissions we might need. The Council is going to be delighted that someone is going to do something with this building that's been vacant for far too long."

"What else?" Chef Claire said.

"You'll need to set aside a portion of your wine cellar for some of my personal collection."

"Here we go," I said, laughing.

"Nothing major," my mother said. "I'll just need enough room for a few cases. I plan on eating here often, and my dinner guests tend to be, let's call them, upscale clientele."

Josie laughed.

"Yes, we know, Mom."

"And I'd like to have a table that I can call my own. I'll let you know which one as soon as the renovations are complete."

"You got it, Mrs. C.," Chef Claire shaking her head at the wonder that was my mother. "Anything else?"

"No, that's it," my mother said. "I'm pretty low maintenance."

All three of us let that one pass without comment.

"Josie and I also have one stipulation," I said. "During the season, we'd like the verandah area outside to be dog-friendly. And during the winter, we'd like the same thing in the bar."

"Absolutely," Chef Claire said. "Actually, I've always wanted to include a dog menu. But I'm not sure that will fly with the Health Department."

"You let me worry about that, my dear," my mother said, waving away Chef Claire's concern. "I can't even count the number of favors the health inspector owes me."

"Old friend, Mom?"

"No, dear," she said, flashing me a quick smile. "He's not that old at all."

Chef Claire looked at Josie and me.

"How would the corporation be structured?"

"We were thinking about a sixty, twenty, twenty split," I said. "Of course, the sixty percent is yours."

"I still don't know why I should get twenty percent," Josie said.

"You get twenty percent because we're business partners," I said to Josie for what was probably the tenth time. "It what's we do."

"All right," Josie said, catching the tone in my voice. "I'll let it go."

"Good. But just remember that you don't eat for free," I said, laughing. "If we allow that, we'll be closed down in six months."

"Funny," Josie said.

"So what do you say?" I said to Chef Claire.

"I'm worried about the winters," she said.

"You worry too much," Josie said.

"So you're saying that I'll get used to them?" Chef Claire said.

"No, absolutely not. They're brutal," Josie said. "I'm just saying that you worry too much."

For some reason, my mother and I found Josie's comment a lot funnier than Chef Claire did.

"All you'll need to do is make sure you get some staff you trust enough to run things if you want to take some time off," my mother said. "And when you do, you can come spend some time with me at my place in Grand Cayman." She glared at me. "If you did, you'd be the first."

"What can I say, Mom? Our dogs need us."

"And I don't?" my mother said, holding a hand to her chest.

"Nice try, Mom," I said, laughing.

Actually, Josie and I had been talking about taking her up on her offer. I'd seen the photos and the place was magnificent. I looked at Chef Claire.

"So?"

"Okay," Chef Claire said, nodding. "I'm in. But it's going to be a ton of work."

"Yes, indeed," my mother said, reaching into her purse and removing several business cards. "Here's the card for a local architect that has done some work for me. Here's one for a local construction company that I highly recommend. The other cards are for people you might need for kitchen equipment, furniture, and all the other usual suspects."

Chef Claire stared down at the handful of business cards.

"Thanks, Mrs. C.," Chef Claire said.

"No problem, my dear," my mother said as she looked around. "I think Memorial Day would be a great weekend to open."

I knew she wasn't joking.

"Okay," Chef Claire said.

"Welcome to the family," I said, laughing.

"We'll need to come up with a name," Josie said.

"Well, since I'm Chef Claire, you're the Chandlers, and Josie's last name is Court, how about we just call it C's?"

We thought about it, and I decided it had a nice ring to it.

"I love it," Josie said.

"It's perfect," I said.

"Let's hope everything is as easy as that was," Chef Claire said.

"Okay, I think we're finished here," my mother said. "If I remember correctly, Suzy, you said something about buying me breakfast."

"I did, didn't I? Breakfast sounds great. What do you say, Josie?"

"I could eat."

My mother locked the door, and we headed for our cars. I noticed the new car my mother was driving. It was a black on black top of the line Audi."

"Did you get another new car, Mom?"

"Yes, darling. After my recent breakup, I decided my old one had far too many bad memories associated with it."

"Mom, you had it for maybe a month. How many memories did you have time to create?"

"Enough. And all of them were bad."

I nodded. It was hard to argue with her logic on that one.

"Where did you get it?"

"From Dirk, of course," she said climbing into the car.

"After what that guy did to you, you went and bought another car from him?"

"No, darling. After what he did to me, and what he knew I could do to him, he *gave* me the car."

"You threatened to blackmail him?"

"Of course not, darling," she said, starting the engine. "It was a simple case of what I like to call humiliation-fueled payback."

"Tomato, tomahto?"

"Exactly. I'll see you at the Café."

She roared off and left me standing in the middle of the road. Josie approached, and we stared at the car until it turned and disappeared from view.

"You know, now that he's back on the market, maybe I should hook up with Dirk," Josie said.

"I don't think Dirk ever really left the market," I said, playing along with her.

"You've got a point there."

"But if you did, you'd have to figure out a way to catch him cheating on you, right?" I said.

"Yeah."

"I don't know, Josie. It sounds like an awful lot of work."

"Yeah, you're probably right," she said. "But I'd kill for that car."

I laughed and then we rejoined Chef Claire and drove to the Café and ate ourselves silly.

Epilogue

It took a while for the shock of John's arrest to dissipate. Upon hearing the news, no one in town believed it at first, but when people heard the full story, everyone was extremely disappointed. Some, like Josie and me, were heartbroken. But after a few weeks of constant chatter around town, gradually everyone moved on, and our attention shifted to Thanksgiving that was rapidly approaching. Christmas and the full onset of winter would soon follow, but judging from the light snow that was falling this morning as the sun appeared in the early morning sky, winter might have decided to make a relatively early appearance this year.

"How do you think Chef Claire does her cranberries?" Josie said.

"Really? Given everything that's gone on recently, that's what's on your mind?" I said, adjusting our trolling speed to four miles an hour.

"I'm tired of thinking about all the other stuff," Josie said.

She was sitting across from me out of the wind as much as possible wearing her parka, and a wool ski hat pulled down low over her forehead. Her gloves were wrapped around a cup of steaming hot chocolate. Chloe was on her lap and doing her best to hide in and under Josie's parka.

"Chloe, you're such a baby," I said, laughing. "You're the one with a fur coat."

"It's freezing out here, and you know it," Josie said, taking a sip of hot chocolate.

"Yeah, it certainly is," I said, zipping my coat. "But this is the last time we'll be on the River this year, so let's try to enjoy it."

The boat was scheduled to be pulled from the water tomorrow and put into storage until the last bit of ice disappeared next spring. Josie and I always made it a point to have a final day on the River each year, but given recent events, we'd been busy and had almost missed our window of opportunity. Our last boat ride each year was usually held on a glorious fall afternoon and was organized around a water picnic involving several boats filled with friends. This year we were flying solo and so far the morning was highlighted by me trying to catch a Muskie while Josie whined and pounded hot chocolate.

It was already clear that this day wasn't going to become an annual tradition.

I glanced back at my fishing rod inserted into a holder attached to the stern. My rod remained stationary, and I assumed that my Muskie count would remain at zero. And I'm not talking about this morning. I've been fishing for them for years, but have never caught a single one.

That's a bit fat zero for those of you keeping score.

And as someone who prides herself as a good fisherman, it was a sore spot.

I refused to believe that it was that hard to catch one.

"Did you see the story yesterday about John's trial starting next month?" Josie said, refilling her mug.

"Yeah, it sounds like there wasn't much his lawyers could do to slow it down," I said. "The recording has him confessing to the two murders as well as drug smuggling. He's pretty much convicted himself."

"I still can't believe it," Josie said.

"Yeah, it's a sad situation," I whispered.

"Why do you think he just kept talking on the boat that day?"

"He didn't think we'd ever have the chance to tell anybody," I said. "He underestimated us."

"No, he underestimated you. I thought you'd lost your mind," Josie said. "But you were amazing, Suzy."

My face flushed, and my eyes welled with tears as they had most days since the events on the boat. I felt some degree of pride about solving the murders, but I was also sad, even sometimes ashamed, for having done that to someone who'd once been a very close friend.

As if reading my mind, Josie said, "He would have killed us, Suzy." She stared off into the distance. "It's hard to imagine doing that to anyone, much less three good friends."

"As my mother says, somewhere along life's pathway, John lost his soul, then he lost his way."

"Really? Your mother said that?" Josie said, glancing at me over the top of her mug as she took a sip.

"She's recently started reading Eastern philosophy," I said.

"Mid-life crisis?"

"She's dating her yoga instructor," I said.

"Unbelievable," Josie said, laughing. "I just love your mother."

"Yeah, me too," I said, nodding.

"So is this new boyfriend a keeper?"

"No, Mom says he's more of the catch and release variety," I said. "But she's having fun, and she looks great. I'm thinking about starting to do yoga."

Josie snorted.

"I wish you wouldn't do that," I said, glaring at her.

"Sorry. It's an involuntary response."

"Well, it's not an attractive quality," I said. "But I need to start doing something physical. I've gained five pounds since the start of summer. And winter is when I can pack it on if I'm not careful."

"You look great," Josie said. "And you needed to put a few pounds on."

"You really think so?"

"Absolutely."

"Thanks. Have you gained any weight since Chef Claire moved in?"

"Not an ounce," she said, shaking her head.

"How is that possible?"

"Suzy, we spend our days taking care of dozens of dogs, and we probably walk five to ten miles a day while we're at work. Not to mention all the stuff we lug around. Just keep taking care of our dogs and the weight will take care of itself."

"Are you sure?"

"I am," she said, leaning back in her seat to give Chloe the room she needed to readjust her sleeping position. "At least for a couple more years."

"Then what?"

"Then we either cut back on the food or we start panicking."

I laughed long and hard at that one.

Then I decided the Muskie weren't interested in what I had to offer and I put the boat in neutral. I put my fishing rod away for the season then stretched out on the padded cushion that ran along the transom. Chloe decided she wanted some time with her Mama and jumped off Josie's lap and hopped up onto the cushion and tucked herself against me out of the wind. She licked my hand and fell asleep as I stroked her fur.

We sat quietly for several minutes in the cold and wind. Despite the weather, the River was beautiful at this time of year and the silence this morning was overpowering.

"The last boat ride of the year always makes me a bit melancholy," I said.

"Spring is just around the corner," Josie said.

"What?"

"Of course it's a very long corner," she said.

"You don't have to wait until spring to get back on the River," I said.

"Suzy, you can try to sell me on it until you're blue in the face," Josie said. "Which I'm sure it will be about an hour after you start. But there is no way I'm going ice fishing."

"You don't know what you're missing," I said.

"Yes, I do. Frostbite and brandy."

We both heard the boat before we saw it. It soon appeared in the distance, and when the driver saw us, the boat veered toward us and slowed as it approached. Jackson waved, and we saw Sluggo in the seat next to him. Josie caught the side of Jackson's new boat and tied it off against ours.

"Fishing for Muskie?" Jackson said.

"She was," Josie said. "I'm drinking hot chocolate. You want a cup?"

"No, I'm good, thanks," he said. "I'm just taking the boat out for a final run. But I think it's a bit cold for Sluggo out here, so I'm heading back."

At the mention of Sluggo, Chloe perked up and barked. She put her paws up on the side of the boat and peered at her friend in the other boat. Josie laughed and lifted her up and handed her to Jackson. He set Chloe down, and the dogs spent a few minutes getting reacquainted before huddling next to each other under Jackson's seat.

"I stopped by your new place yesterday to have a look," Jackson said.

"So you were snooping," I said.

"I'm the Chief of Police. I don't snoop," Jackson said. "It's going to look great when it's finished."

"Yes, it is," I said. "We're pretty excited about it."

"Everybody is excited about having Chef Claire in town," he said. "You know, I've been thinking about asking her out."

Josie and I looked at each other and smiled.

"What?" Jackson said.

"I think it's a great idea, Jackson," I said. "But you better hurry."

"Why?"

"Because Freddie told us the same thing yesterday," Josie said.

"I can't believe it," Jackson said. "I ran into him last night, and he didn't say a thing about it. That little sneak. We were even talking about Chef Claire at one point."

"Oooh, there's some competition for Chef Claire's heart," I said, laughing.

"Let the games begin," Josie said. "And you were worried that we might get bored this winter."

"Not anymore," I said, laughing. "And since she's staying with us, we're going to have a front row seat."

"And they're both coming for Thanksgiving dinner," Josie said. "This is perfect."

"It's nice to know that I can always count on you two for support."

He leaned down to pick up Chloe and handed her back to Josie. Chloe hopped back up on the cushion next to me. I pulled a plastic bag of cookies out of my pocket, gave her two, and tossed the bag to Jackson. We watched as he fed the final three to Sluggo one at a time.

"I visited Alice the other day," Jackson said, rubbing Sluggo's head.

"How is she doing?" I said.

"She's a mess," he said. "But I guess that's what can happen when you lose sight of what's really important."

I let it go. Alice was going away for a very long time, and Jackson was devastated by the thought that his former summer intern had come very close to killing him. But nothing we said could change anything, so I stayed quiet.

"I need to run," Jackson said, starting his boat.

"It's a great boat," Josie said.

"I'm still in shock," he said. "I've never won anything before in my life."

A few weeks ago, we were finally able to conduct the raffle for the boat that should have been given away the night that Roger the Engineer was killed. To the surprise and delight of everyone in town, Jackson had been the lucky winner.

"Where are you going in such a hurry?" I said, grinning at Josie.

"Oh, nowhere," he said. "I guess I'll head back into town and maybe grab some breakfast."

"And swing by to say hi to Chef Claire?" Josie said.

"You guys aren't going to let this go, are you?"

"Not a chance," I said.

"Thanks for the warning," he said, pushing his boat away from ours, and heading off in the direction of the town dock.

"This is going to be fun to watch," Josie said.

"It certainly is," I said. "Fifty bucks says Jackson gets a second date with her before Freddie."

"You're on," Josie said. "But you have to agree to let it play out. No interfering."

"Would I do something like that?" I said, doing my best to sound offended.

Josie shook her head and stared at Jackson's boat that had almost disappeared.

"You know, it's funny how life works sometimes. And how quickly things can change. One minute Jackson is at death's door, the next he's fully recovered and lucky enough to win a hundred thousand dollar boat in a raffle."

"Yeah, I guess life can be funny like that," I said, looking off into the distance.

"Suzy?"

"Yeah."

"I don't know how you did it, but I think you had something to do with Jackson winning that boat."

"Why on earth would you think something like that?"

It started to snow and the flurries soon intensified.

"Look at that," I said. "It's starting to come down hard. And it's cold enough for it to accumulate. Let's get out of here and go grab some breakfast."

"I could eat."

I started the boat, and I hunched down in my seat to avoid the wind. Boating season on the River was officially over. I slowly headed for town. Just because the season was over didn't mean I couldn't squeeze every last drop out of it.

I felt Josie staring at me but focused on my driving.

"Suzy?"

"Yeah," I said, giving her a quick glance.

"You rigged the raffle, didn't you?"

"Maybe."

"You're unbelievable."

"I have my moments."

Here's an excerpt from the next installment in B.R. Snow's *Thousand Islands Doggy Inn Mystery* series:

THE CASE OF THE CAGED COCKERS

Chapter 1

On a frigid, snowy Thursday, Thanksgiving came and went. The entire day was filled with great conversation in the company of good friends in a warm house and a menu that even the all-too-modest Chef Claire had to admit was one of her best. Friday's dinner was a repeat of the previous day's *turkey with all the fixings* that was as good if not better than the original. Between the two dinners, Josie and I embarked on a wild flurry of snacking that shattered all of our previous records for gluttony and bad table manners that caused my mother, at one point on Friday afternoon, to wonder out loud who the alien was that bore a striking resemblance to the daughter she had raised.

We had dressed for Thanksgiving dinner, but by the time the pumpkin trifle and an apple pie topped with a brandy caramel sauce that was a total knee-buckler were served, Josie and I had swapped out our dinner attire for the snacker pants we were still wearing when the weekend rolled around.

The pants were taking quite a beating this year but seemed to be holding up.

Friday started with a breakfast turkey quiche that disappeared in ten minutes. That was followed later in the day by a turkey sandwich, a bowl of pumpkin trifle, a hot turkey sandwich with gravy, a slice of apple pie, then another sandwich in that order followed by a long nap.

Or as my mother called it; a tryptophan coma.

I had to hand it to her. She was definitely on her game this holiday season.

Friday night, Chef Claire made a turkey gumbo that brought tears to my eyes.

Saturday, she made two different kinds of turkey soup. One was a traditional version; the other was a rustic Italian tomato bread soup with homemade turkey sausage. Josie and I were still debating which one was better, but since there was still half a pot left of each, we weren't in any hurry to make a final decision.

On Sunday night, I hit the wall and was officially turkeyed out. Josie had agreed, but I think she lied to me because the next morning I'd caught her in her office at the Inn gnawing on a turkey leg.

Now I was sitting at the dinner table across from Josie and wondering aloud how was it possible for me to be hungry. Chef Claire came in from the kitchen carrying a tray filled with bite-sized appetizers that were steaming hot. She set them down on the table, and I stared down at the tray, then looked up at Chef Claire.

"I've wanted to test this idea out for a long time," Chef Claire said.

"Well, if you're looking for two guinea pigs to try it out on, you've come to the right place," Josie said.

"What are they?" I said, staring lovingly at the fresh baked objects that were no more than two inches long.

"Try one, and then you tell me," Chef Claire said.

Needing no encouragement, I picked one up and popped it into my mouth. As I chewed, a flood of memories raced through my head.

"That's incredible," I said. "How did you do that?"

Chef Claire beamed with pride and selected one from the tray. Josie followed suit. As she chewed, she stared at Chef Claire.

"I call them One Bite Thanksgiving," Chef Claire said.

"Good name," I said, nodding. "Because that's exactly what they are. I swear that one bite reminded me of Thanksgiving dinners from years ago."

"How is this possible?" Josie said, reaching for another.

Chef Claire grabbed one of the one-bite wonders and carefully cut it in half.

"I made a Chinese dumpling dough, and then I layered a thin slice of turkey, stuffing, mashed and sweet potatoes, and cranberry, then put a dollop of gravy over the top and sealed them tight. I did these on the stovetop, but I have another batch steaming at the moment."

I picked up one of the halves and examined it carefully. How it was possible to recreate an entire holiday dinner in an object that was less than an inch high was beyond my comprehension abilities, but I certainly wasn't going to argue the point.

I decided to postpone my earlier decision about being turkeyed out for another day and helped myself to another. Just as I was reaching for my fifth one, my phone rang. I wiped my hands and mouth and answered the call.

"This is Suzy. A delivery at this time of night?" I looked at Josie. She shook her head. "No, I'm sorry. I don't think we ordered anything for delivery tonight… What do you mean the contents are expiring?"

I frowned, and Josie sat back in her chair listening closely.

"Yes, I see… Who is this?"

The call ended abruptly, and I set my phone down on the table.

"That was odd," I said. "Whoever that was said there's been a delivery at the Inn and it's outside the door. And they said we should hurry up and get it because the contents are expiring."

"That is odd," Josie said. "It's so cold out there I can't imagine what could possibly spoil before morning."

"Yeah," I said, starting to reach for another of the appetizers. Then I stopped. "Unless it's alive."

"Like a dog," Josie said, scrambling to her feet.

We raced outside and headed down the stairs until we reached the back entrance of the Inn. There was nothing on the back porch, so we raced around the side until we reached the front. Near the door was a cardboard box wrapped in a flimsy cotton blanket. Josie knelt down and pulled the blanket back. Tears immediately welled in my eyes when I heard the soft whimpers coming from inside the box.

I opened the front door and turned the thermostat way up as Josie carried the box into one of the examination rooms.

"This is bad," she said, carefully reaching into the box. "There are six of them. They can't be more than four weeks old."

"Can you save them?" I said.

"Well, we're certainly going to do everything we possibly can," Josie said. "Grab a bunch of blankets and towels."

She pulled out her phone and located the number.

"Sammy, it's Josie. I need you here now. Do you know where Jill is?...That's great. Bring her along. Get over here immediately."

She ended the call and refocused on what was inside the cardboard box. I returned with the blankets, and she spread them out one at a time on the floor and gently placed one of the puppies on a blanket and wrapped it loosely. She repeated the process until all six puppies were safely cocooned.

"Okay," she said. "Remember to remind Sammy and Jill when they get here that they can't rub or pet them until we're sure frostbite hasn't set in."

"But hypothermia has set in, right?"

"Yeah, let's hope that's as bad as it gets. But I'm worried about one of the front legs on the little guy on the left. He's showing signs of some serious tissue damage."

"You mean he might lose the leg?"

"It's a possibility, Suzy," she said. "But for now let's focus on making sure he doesn't lose his life. We need to deal with the hypothermia first."

I stared down at the dazed expressions on the cocker spaniel's faces and heard their whimpers as I continued to fight back the tears. A few minutes later, Sammy and Jill raced inside the exam room and glanced down at the six puppies wrapped in blankets on the floor.

"You got here fast," Josie said, cradling two of the puppies to her chest. "Both of you take a puppy and hold it like this."

Sammy and Jill each cradled a puppy, and I picked up the other two. I briefly outlined what had happened as the four of us sat on the tile floor and did our best to get the puppies' core temperature up.

"Thanks for coming in," I said.

"No problem," Sammy said, glancing at Jill. "We just happened to be watching a movie together tonight. I guess it was lucky that we were in the same place when you called."

Josie looked at me and grinned. Sammy and Jill had been seeing each other for at least three months, but they continued to believe that no one had figured that out yet. The main ingredient in a grilled cheese sandwich was a better-kept secret. This seemed like as good a time as any to pop that balloon.

"Sammy," I said.

"Yeah."

"We know."

"Know what?"

"About you and Jill," I said.

"You do?" Sammy said, glancing at Jill.

"I told you," Jill said, glancing nervously back and forth between Josie and me. "I'm sorry we didn't say anything. We weren't sure how you guys would react."

"Has your relationship impacted your work?" Josie said.

"No," Jill said.

"Or the way you treat the dogs?" Josie said.

"Absolutely not," Sammy said.

"Well, there you go," Josie said, glancing down at one of the puppies stirring in her arms. "This little guy is starting to come around. She's licking my hand."

"Mine too," I said.

Josie handed one of the dogs she was holding to Jill and stood, still holding the puppy with the damaged front leg close to her.

"Okay, I think it's safe to slowly remove the blankets," Josie said. "But if they start shivering again when you do, immediately wrap them back up. Suzy and Sammy, I need you to carefully check each puppy for potential frostbite. You're looking for signs of tissue discoloration, blisters, or swelling. And if they react in pain when you touch them, make a note of that area. If you find any of those symptoms, you'll need to run some warm water no hotter than 108 degrees and start by gently patting those spots with the water. Then wrap a dry, warm towel around them. If the spots look particularly damaged, go ahead and put a heating pad wrapped in a towel against it. But you can't rub or pet those spots the way you normally would. Pat, but don't rub."

"Got it," I said, already pulling back one of the blankets to begin my examination. Then I glanced up at Josie. "Where are you going to be?"

"Surgery," Josie whispered. "I'm going to need your help, Jill."

Jill gently set the puppy she was holding down next to Sammy and stood. She followed Josie out of the exam room and headed for the back of the Inn where our surgery area was located. I knew what that meant and felt another round of tears streaming down my cheeks.

"What kind of monster leaves a litter of puppies outside in a box on a cold night like this?" Sammy said, gently rolling one of the puppies over onto its back.

"Actually, Sammy. I think whoever did this was trying to figure out a way to save them," I said.

Sammy thought about what I said for a moment, then refocused on the puppy he was examining.

"But why would they do it anonymously?" he said.

"Now that's a very good question."

CPSIA information can be obtained
at www.ICGtesting.com
Printed in the USA
LVHW051014060721
691900LV00011B/1749

9 781942 691068